THE PARTRIDGE FAMILY
DIGS A WILD NEW SOUND...

Shirley Partridge and the talented kids
who call her "Mom"—Keith, Laurie, Danny,
Christopher and Tracy—are the hottest
rock group on the scene. As such, they
thought they'd heard all the new sounds.

Then they came to the mysterious old house
called "The Haunted Hall" and dug a new one:
"Bo-o-o-o-o-o . . ."

THE PARTRIDGE FAMILY #2: THE HAUNTED HALL

BY MICHAEL AVALLONE

Based on a series created by
Bernard Slade

CURTIS
BOOKS

MODERN LITERARY EDITIONS PUBLISHING COMPANY
NEW YORK, N.Y.

THE PARTRIDGES—

Shirley Partridge—Is "Mom" to five talented children. When the Partridge Family is on tour, it's Shirley who's behind the wheel of the big bus painted in bright psychedelic colors. Her bright strong singing voice has helped make The Partridge Family famous from coast to coast.

Keith Partridge—At seventeen, Shirley's oldest son is "man of the family." A great help to his widowed mother, Keith plays guitar for the group.

Laurie Partridge—Shirley is proud of her pretty teenage daughter. Laurie's singing is part of the Partridge fame.

Danny Partridge—Like his older brother, Danny is great on guitar, and at ten years old, he has a steel-trap mind for business.

Christopher Partridge—Is an eight-year old winner on the drums. He keeps the beat for the group.

Tracy Partridge—Baby of the family, she gives the group plenty of singing support wherever The Partridge Family performs.

Shirley Partridge recorded a song in the family garage with her five talented children—and the family was destined for stardom from the first scratch of a needle! Now they travel in a renovated old school bus painted in bright psychedelic colors. Shirley drives them all over the country in search of life, liberty, and the pursuit of singing engagements.

For the Antonelli Family
-----one and all.

Table of Contents

TO BEGIN WITH 11
OFF TO LARKLAND 19
TURNBULL HOUSE 29
A GOBLIN GIGGLES 41
MORE SOUNDS IN THE NIGHT 49
MORNING AT SATAN HALL 57
THE GREAT JINGO 69
LAURIE'S HEROES 81
A HOUSE IS NOT A BONFIRE 87
DUKE TO THE RESCUE 97
ROCK TIME IN LARKLAND 109
A CALL FOR HELP 119
LARKLAND REMEMBERED 123

TO BEGIN WITH

☐ Sunlight flooded the Partridge family's comfortable living room. It even lightened the thick greenish water of Christopher's turtle tank.

Christopher's mother, Shirley Partridge, peered into its weedy depths. "Christopher Partridge," she said icily to her youngest son, "you find Simon and Garfunkel within the next ten minutes or out they go!"

"But, Mom—"

"Don't Mom me! You had distinct orders not to let those turtles out of the tank. It's feeding time, anyway. Knowing how you enjoy slipping them choice chunks of shrimp and worms—" But she was talking to herself. Christopher had turned and raced up the stairs.

Shirley Partridge sat down and reached for the latest issue of *McCall's*. She planned to enjoy these few hours she had to herself. Keith, Laurie, Danny and Tracy had gone to the high school to watch band practice and maybe sit in for a jam session.

Her musical offspring were now celebrities, but their fame hadn't gone to their heads. They were still nice kids, she thought. Of course Danny would reel off a list of their accomplishments to anyone who would listen, but it wasn't really boasting. Danny was just a practical, ten-year-old redhead. A forty-year-old midget, a Wall Street financier were what their manager, Reuben Kinkaid called him. Danny had kept

Reuben hopping ever since the little redhead had trapped him into listening to their "demo" record which had brought fame and fortune to the Partridge Family. When the record leaped into the Top 40, Shirley bought an old school bus, repainted it, and had driven her talented family all over the country on a singing tour. They played at clubs and filled engagements wherever they were wanted.

Now, with a two-day break between engagements, the family was on the eve of another long cross-country trip—this time to the Larkland Rock Festival, by special request of the Governor of the state. It was the rock fans that had made the Partridges a top singing group attraction.

Christopher was still upstairs and Shirley was still reading when the phone on the coffee table rang.

It was manager Reuben Kinkaid—confident and breezy as usual. (Only Danny Partridge could stop Reuben Kinkaid.)

"And how are my bright stars this golden afternoon?" Reuben asked.

"Not half as shiny as you sound. What happened? Did we top the Beatles in the Top 40?"

Reuben laughed. "Just wanted to tell you I've made all the arrangements for Larkland. You open on Thursday and the governor tells me it's the biggest thing the state has had. Plenty of newspaper, radio and TV coverage. They even got a movie star to come in from the Coast to plug his latest western."

"John Wayne? Christopher will be very happy if it's John Wayne. He's seen *Red River* twenty times on TV, now."

Ruben Kinkaid chuckled.

"Sorry. Duke can't make it this year. But what disappoints one Partridge makes another very happy.

Laurie ought to flip and do handstands and burn up all her old pictures of David McCallum. You listening? How's Jerry Jingo for openers?"

"Honest? Why, that's great. Those motorcycles and his detective movies have made him the hottest thing in pictures. The kids all love him. Appearing with him isn't going to hurt our image at all."

"I should say not," Reuben Kinkaid agreed, rather huffily. "What's more important, he'll draw the crowds. And once they hear you—Oh, I can see the headlines now. I tell you, Shirley, things are getting better all the time."

"Neat-o, as Keith would say. How'd you make out on our hotel arrangements?"

There was a pause.

"Reuben? Are you still there—"

"Still here." The cooler sound of his voice made Shirley frown. "You are going to find this impossible to believe, Shirley."

"No, I won't." Shirley said crisply. "I can believe anything by now. What's the matter?"

"I couldn't get you a decent room in a decent hotel in all of Larkland. City that big, too! There isn't an accommodation left, and I wasn't going to stick you in some motel outside of town."

"Reuben, if you're suggesting that the kids and I sleep in the bus—"

He laughed again. A trifle lamely, she thought.

"Would I do that to you?"

"You sure would. You won't let us fly. I have to keep driving that crate all because you tell me it makes us so colorful. Now tell me, Reuben, and tell me quick—what have you got for us in Larkland?"

He began to explain very carefully, so that she

wouldn't misunderstand him. She listened very politely but his words made her heart sink.

". . . very old mansion. Lovely place, really. On the outskirts of town. Right in the heart of the woods. Just a 20-minute ride from downtown Larkland. You'll love it, the kids will love it, and it won't cost a dime. Some old philanthropist, name of J. Watterson Turnbull, who seems to love musicians of all kinds and grades, is donating it to you for your stay. . . ."

"Oh, Reuben—" she sighed.

"Did I say something wrong?"

"You sure did. It could be the loveliest house in the world but for crying out loud, Reuben. It sounds like no maids, no cooking, no one to make up the beds. I'm a mother and a housewife, all right, but I'm also a hardworking entertainer and the idea of cooking my own meals while we're working doesn't exactly thrill me."

"Now Shirley, you know I take care of you. I've hired a cook, chauffeur, and a housekeeper. Do you think old Reuben Kinkaid would let you down?"

"You'll love this old house. It's a bit off the beaten track but that ought to make it interesting. You can rehearse in the woods and generally have a ball—"

"Wait a minute," Shirley broke in, "This J. Watterson Trumbull—"

"Turnbull. What about him?"

"Well, doesn't he live on the premises? Doesn't he—"

Reuben Kinkaid chuckled.

"Reuben," she said, warningly. "What are you holding back?"

"I was hoping you wouldn't ask. It doesn't change things. Not really. After all, it's in the past. Twenty years ago."

Shirley Partridge set her teeth together.

"Reuben Kinkaid, tell me everything. All of it. What happened twenty years ago?"

He cleared his throat and spoke in a rush.

"Shirley, Mr. Turnbull doesn't live in the house. He's an inmate of a sanitarium in Blue Rapids. You see, twenty years ago he turned into a firebug of some kind and burned down a lot of buildings. So they put him away. But he was a wealthy man without a family. Real wealthy. No heirs. So his lawyers take care of his property. For years now they've wanted to turn his old mansion into a home for the aged or something, but nothing's quite worked out. Meanwhile, no one is living in it. So when I found out about it through the Chamber of Commerce, they thought it a wonderful idea for the Partridges to use it—"

"The poor old man. How terrible. Well, I guess the kids will find it fun. What kind of mansion is it? Tudor? Colonial?"

"It's a mansion," Reuben Kinkaid barked, "and you'll have enough room to float a battleship. Okay, now? What do I know about mansions? I was raised in a housing project."

Shirley laughed.

"Okay, Reuben. Thanks for the mansion. It might just be fun after all. Is it easy to find?"

"I'll send you a map complete with compass and directions."

"You coming to see us at the Festival?" Shirley asked.

"I wouldn't miss it. Take me a day or so to close out a few business matters here in New York and then I'll be out pronto."

"Don't forget to bring out the latest issue of the

Wall Street Journal. Danny's very worried about his Pepsi-Cola stock."

"I'll bet. So long, Shirley. See you in Larkland. And knock 'em dead."

He hung up.

Keith, Laurie, Danny and Tracy, came trooping in soon afterward and Shirley told them all about Reuben Kinkaid's phone call. Right away, everybody was excited.

"Now that's what I call living in the style we should be accustomed to," Danny Partridge said.

"I'd call it *relevant* to our position," teen-ager Laurie smiled, her lovely face radiant. "We should always have first class accommodations."

"Oh, definitely," said Keith, the oldest. "And we'll have a star on every door."

Baby-of-the-family, Tracy, her pixie face aglow, clapped her hands. "Goodie! I hope my star is bright gold."

"Go on upstairs, Tracy," Shirley smiled at the small girl. "Tell Christopher to stop playing with Simon and Garfunkel. He's going to wear them out."

"You can't wear out a turtle," Danny was very firm on that point. "They can survive an earthquake. The biggest disasters—"

"Maybe so," Shirley Partridge said grimly, "but I can't say the same for mothers. Now, all of you. March upstairs, get washed and if you're all nice to me and listen to what I tell you, maybe—just maybe—I'll take you all out for dinner in a fancy restaurant. What do you say to that idea?"

There was a resounding chorus of approval.

Shirley Partridge had no way of knowing that the Wheel of Life was about to take a weird and terrifying spin for herself and her children: that their stay in the old dark house in the woods was to prove altogether ghostly and ghastly.

Reuben Kinkaid had not told her *everything*. But who believes in haunted houses, anyway?

OFF TO LARKLAND

☐ Rain pattered off their wildly painted bus as Shirley Partridge grimly maneuvered along the highway. The downpour had been sudden, beginning soon after they had left home, and continuing steadily. Shirley was tired. In another two hours they'd be in Larkland, but another two hours of this driving seemed like ages to her. She shifted uncomfortably at the wheel, trying to ignore the dizzy swing of the windshield wipers. Back and forth. Left, right, left, right, one, two, one, two. You could almost set it to music. *Me, you, me, you* . . .

The kids must have had the same idea because Keith suddenly cleared his throat and began to sing in his firm, clear tenor voice.

"Raindrops falling on my bus . . . just like the sky was crying, trying to tell us . . . something's got to give . . ."

He kept on going, parodying the Burt Bacharach song from the movie *Butch Cassidy And The Sundance Kid*. Not as good as Mr. Bacharach, of course, but Keith was doing all right. Laurie and Danny were chiming in, too, with rhythmic emphasis and warmth. Christopher was still pouting about having to leave Simon and Garfunkel behind, and Tracy was playing with her doll. On long bus rides, Tracy was a regular little Mommie.

The kids suddenly ended the song with a musical flourish and began talking about movies.

"Butch and the Kid had the right idea," Danny said. "Robbing all those banks the way they did. In those days the capitalists themselves were nothing but crooks, robbing the poor. But they lacked organization. Management—"

Keith said. "It was a good movie. Nobody cares what you think of their way of doing things."

"Westerns. War films." Laurie made a face. "Don't you boys ever think of anything else? Life has to have more meaning than cowboys and gunslingers. There are so many more things that are relevant."

"Yeah?" Danny challenged. "Name one."

"Love," Laurie said firmly. "Real love."

Keith looked at her, grinning.

"Your boy friend Jerry Jingo makes a lot of westerns and war films. What about that? And so does Steve McQueen. And you think he's something, don't you? We know you do! How about that?"

Laurie tilted her chin.

"Jerry Jingo is *not* my boy friend. And just because I happen to think he's so excessively manly and handsome and good, doesn't mean I change my stand about his pictures. Someday he will make a beautiful film. About love and a man's purpose in life. Just you wait and see."

Keith turned away to stare at the rain slapping against the window. "Well, you just act grown-up when we see him at Larkland and don't fall all over his neck like some silly kid. Heck—he's not much older than I am and I don't want you embarrassing the family by acting like an amateur. We're in Show Biz too, you know."

Two pink spots appeared in Laurie's smooth face.

"He's a star. A very big star. And he's not even twenty yet and he's a Scorpio which means he's sensitive and just because a lot of sensitive girls have responded to his *charisma*—"

"His what?" Danny cracked.

"Maybe she means he burned his draft card," Keith said with a straight face.

Danny snorted. "Yeah, Laurie. Why isn't he in the army?"

"Or Canada even," Keith laughed, now.

"Oh!" Laurie Partridge was absolutely livid, now. "*You!*"

With that, she tilted her chin in the air, scrunched up in her seat, folded her arms and glared out at the rain beating against the windows. Keith and Danny exchanged grins, and Christopher expressed his feelings about Mom's decision not to pack two turtles along by alternately sticking out his tongue in the direction of Shirley's blonde head and crossing his eyes.

In her own quiet corner of the bus, close to the front and her mother, Laurie's thoughts were playing leap-frog. She was going from acute rage with Keith and Danny to mingled emotions of excitement and worry about Larkland.

Images of Jerry Jingo—his serious blue eyes, curling sideburns, and long black hair, danced in her mind. Gee. A real talent. He had died so beautifully in the last scene of *Watch Out For Charlie*. And wasn't he just something else in *Love My Green Beret?*

And he was about twenty! Exactly the right age for her.

And she'd be seeing him in no time at all, really. Perhaps tomorrow, even!

Her heart flapped with excitement. How could

Mom have been so calm when she announced that they would be sharing the bill at the Larkland Rock Festival with none other than Jerry Jingo? As if he were just another star, another performer!

By late afternoon lightning flashed in the northern sky, but the follow-up thunder sounded far away. Huge winds had come on, chasing the rain away, and driving had become easier. Shirley heaved a sigh of relief.

They were nearing Larkland now. She had passed the identifying signposts and landmarkers which Reuben Kinkaid had crudely drawn on his "map." He instructed her to take the left fork off the long road leading down into Larkland. It was fairly good for a side road, but curving as a snake, and bordered by dark cypress trees on either side. Despite the dark skies and the coming of nightfall, Shirley could still see ahead fairly clearly.

Now clusters of tidy brick houses appeared along the roadway. Larkland's outskirts were rather pretty, she decided. It was only when they had left the houses behind them that she consulted Reuben's map once more. She was sure she hadn't lost the way, and she hadn't. A quick glance at the map heartened her. Kinkaid's instructions were to stay on this road, heading south, until she saw a right-hand turn at iron-barred gates. And, *voila*—the Partridges would be at the mansion of J. Watterson Turnbull.

The road was darker now, thanks to the tall cypress trees. Shirley slowed the bus to avoid the increasing number of rough spots in the road. It didn't look well-traveled at all. Shirley began to worry just a bit. She felt all alone in the world now because all the kids were dozing in the bus, as they always did when they had traveled for a very long stretch. Only Simone was awake. And that scruffy character was lying in the center aisle, worrying a rubber ball.

Two miles more, and all she could see was more road, more trees and more countryside. Not a sign of life.

Finally, as she was about to stop and recheck Reuben's map, convinced she had come the wrong way, something glittered up ahead.

Something black, yet shiny.

She slowed the bus and then stepped on the brake, bringing the big vehicle to a stop. She could have driven right on by if she hadn't spied the rain-washed metal spikes of an ancient wrought-iron gate. It was the entrance to the J. Watterson Turnbull mansion.

Shirley took a deep breath and peered out through the side door of the bus at the gate. What a spooky sight! No lights ahead. Not even a glimpse of the house. Just a dark, steep driveway.

There was just enough room to park the bus at the gate. They would have to walk to the house. Shirley sighed. It would be a good half-hour drive from here into the city of Larkland. She tried not to frown. Still, she was glad the trip was done. And a hot meal and a warm bath and a good night's sleep in such peaceful surroundings ought to put them back in shape. There was not even a cricket chirping in the brush. The place was as quiet as a—a cemetery!

She shook herself, eased out from the wheel, and turned to wake up her family.

She walked down the aisle, gently shaking one sleeper after the other, into wakefulness. Simone forgot about the rubber ball and began to yip delightedly. Shirley didn't mind her barking. It had a [...] friendly sound. And it would help wake up the kids[...]

"Last stop," she called out, gaily. "Last one out's a rotten musician. And a square."

That did it. The kids all yawned and stretched awake. Keith blinked the sleep from his eyes and peered through the window. The high iron-spiked gate of the Turnbull property was the first thing to greet his eyes.

"Where are we?" He yawned again.

"Mr. Turnbull's" Shirley answered, wondering what the house would be like. Tracy put down her doll and reached for her shoes. Christopher nudged Danny, and pointed to Simone who was now lying on her back with her four paws in the air. Danny couldn't have cared less. He was now hungry, thirsty, and cross, in that order. He had been dreaming that he had just cornered the market on cassettes during a Wall Street panic and the dream had been so pleasant he wanted to go back to it.

Laurie wiped at the window as if she could clear the drops on the outside glass. She could only glimpse the eerie, rather frightening grounds beyond the gate.

And yet, there was something very familiar about the sight. She had the feeling that she had visited the place before. Then it came to her, and she let out a whoop. The sound was so sudden and loud in the dim bus that her mother jumped and stared at her.

So did the others.

"And pray tell," Shirley asked, "what does that mean?"

Laurie grinned.

"This place. It suddenly occurred to me that it's exactly like another place we see on television."

"Like what place?"

"Like Collins House. You know—on the *Dark Shadows* program."

Shirley Partridge shuddered. "That's a cheery thought. *I'm* trying to think of it as something out of *Green Acres*."

Everybody laughed and Laurie's thought was soon forgotten in the bustle of leaving the bus and going inside a warm and comfortable house.

Still, Shirley wished Laurie hadn't mentioned *Dark Shadows*. There was something very very creepy about J. Watterson Turnbull's mansion in the heart of the lonely woods. Shirley didn't believe in ghosts or superstitions but she did believe in atmosphere—and this property of Mr. Turnbull's, whatever it might turn out to be, had almost *too* much.

Shirley and the kids scrambled down from the bus and walked to the great entranceway looming above the trees and shrubs and vines. It was getting darker every second. The racing gloomy skies seemed to carry some kind of ominous portent of their own. The wind was whistling through the trees and the leafy branches were making weird sounds. There was a swift tingling drip-drip-drip of rain-drops from the wet leaves overhead.

Laurie Partridge felt thrilled to the marrow of her bones. It was all so new and exciting and mysterious. She imagined herself in the role of Jane Eyre, the beautiful young governess coming to visit Rochester's great, dark house. Or maybe this place would be like *Wuthering Heights*. "Hee-ath-cliffe!" she called sadly, and under her breath.

There was just no telling what dark romance and thrills lay beyond these high iron gates. The world of the future could open up for her just like *that!* And if there just happened to be a tall, darkly handsome man in the Turnbull mansion—

But, for Laurie Partridge, just as for *Jane Eyre*, the worst was yet to come.

Had she but known!

TURNBULL HOUSE

☐ As her mother and the rest of the kids squeezed between the iron bars of the gate and hurried forward, Laurie tagged behind. Everyone was laughing, kidding around, and making funny remarks. But Laurie, her overnight bag in one hand and her pocketbook under her other arm, walked slowly. Even her lively imagination was completely overwhelmed by the sight of the house that loomed ahead of them. Seen through the gnarled old trees, it was like something from a horror movie and TV show. In fear and excitement, Laurie followed the others along a winding stone path to the front door.

The old dark house was enormous—bigger than any place she had ever seen before.

A long roof, broken every ten yards or so by jutting gables and spooky-looking towers stood outlined against the darkening skies just above the forest of trees. Creepy dormer windows, all latticed and trellised, jutted out, each one of them showing some kind of heavy drapery. In the half-light, the huge archway with its heavy twin columns shone like a marble tombstone. Not a single light shone from the dark, stony structure. With night approaching rapidly, Turnbull House was anything but a cheery roadside motel.

Laurie drifted up to the group at the front door, just as her mother lifted the heavy brass doorknocker in both hands. It was shaped like a brass monkey, and when it clanged down against the heavy panels, a hollow, almost deafening roar reverberated somewhere inside the house.

Keith snickered. "Two to one Count Dracula answers the door."

"Uh uh," Danny disagreed. "Lurch. It has to be Lurch."

"Yes," Christopher said very seriously. "This is the sort of place the Addams Family would live in."

"But not the Partridge Family," Shirley said firmly. "Now, stop clowning around, all of you. It's probably like an old English castle inside. With thick rugs and a cheery fireplace—"

Before she could finish her sentence, there was a sudden noisy thud of heavy bolts being shot back. One of the big double doors swept open. Each Partridge, even Keith, took a quick, backward step, their eyes fixed on the door.

Suddenly, Laurie's heart skipped three measures. Somewhere in her head a thousand guitars began to play.

Then her young brother, Christopher blurted "Gee whiz! It's only a *man!*"

Back home in her bedroom, Laurie Partridge's walls were thickly pinned with glossy photos of Clint Eastwood, David McCallum, Dustin Hoffman, Steve McQueen, Michael Caine and Jack Lord. But now suddenly, in the twinkling of an eye, out of nowhere, in one mind-boggling moment, was *reality*. Here was *something else!*

Standing on the threshold of Turnbull Mansion, one hand on the door the other on his hip, was a tall, lean and handsome young man. Not even Paul McCartney was so dreamy.

"Crazy," the man said, his black eyes sweeping over all of them. He was almost smiling.

Mom took charge, as she always did.

"Hello. We're the Partridges. I hope you were expecting us—"

"Like what for?" the young man said, still holding the door but not making a move toward letting them in. Behind his broad back, Laurie could see the dim atmosphere of a long corridor of some kind. A knight's suit of armor threw a shadow acoss the doorway.

"Well," Shirley said, trying not to get angry. "Didn't you get a call from a Mr. Kinkaid, Reuben Kinkaid, that we'd be staying here? You see, we're musicians here for the Larkland Festival—"

The young man shook his head, but he looked amused.

"Phone's been dead. All day. The storm. No cat named Kinkaid meowed in this direction."

"Look," Shirley said, still controlling her anger. "We've been driving a long time. We're damp and cold and tired. Now, if you're the caretaker or whatever, I'm sure you can take my word for it. We do have the right to stay here. The Chamber of Commerce arranged it, you see."

"Sure. I see." The young man suddenly stepped back and pulled the door open wide. "Yeah. I'm the caretaker. I'll take your word for it. You don't look like the kind of lady who would lie to a guy. Sure, you come on in and make yourself at home—"

"Thank you," Shirley answered shortly. "Come on, kids. In you go. We'll straighten this out as soon as we can—"

As Keith, Danny, Christopher, Tracy, and Simone quickly hurried into the house, Laurie was the last to enter. The young man was still at the door.

"Hi," he murmured in her ear as she went by.

Unable to speak, Laurie joined her family in the hall of the strange house.

Now it was apparent that there was no electric lighting of any kind. Flickering candles burned steadily in wall niches on either side of the hall, and glowed on the tall suit of armor. The Partridge Family huddled in the great hall, casting apprehensive glances all about them. The young man closed the front door. It thudded hollowly in the vastness of the house. Shirley turned to him.

"No electricity?" she asked.

"The storm cut everything out. But there's lots of candles. Big, too. Burn for hours."

"That's nice."

Laurie stole up to her mother's elbow and turned to look at the beautiful doorman. He smiled back at her, his eyes twinkling.

Simone made small whimpering noises. Tracy and Christopher huddled together, but Keith and Danny exchanged amused glances. It was all kind of fun to them, then.

"Well," Shirley tried to speak cheerfully. "About time for introductions. I'm Mrs. Partridge and these are my children. Keith—" She reeled off their names, and the young man nodded to each member of the brood. But his glance lingered on Laurie, who was introduced last.

"I'm very pleased to make your acquaintance," Laurie said stiffly. The young man waved a hand in short salute.

"Likewise. Call me Duke. All my friends do."

"Well, Duke," Shirley said, "If you'll show us where the rooms are, we'd like to get settled in. And if there's any kind of a meal you could put together for us, it would be appreciated. I know everybody's starved."

Duke shook his head very slowly.

Shirley swallowed nervously. "What does that mean?"

"I told you. I didn't know you were coming. Nobody phoned. This place is closed up most of the time. I just come in once in awhile to polish the silver and generally keep things ship-shape. There's some canned goods in the kitchen—maybe a loaf of bread or two or three. But beyond that—" He shrugged.

Shirley's visions of a pleasant stay in this house as they prepared for the Larkland Rock Festival vanished in a flash—a purple flash of mingled disappointment and rage. How was she supposed to get six people ready for a show in a set-up like this one?

"But that's ridiculous!" Laurie felt she had to take Mom's side. "Our manager promised us everything would be ready for us."

"Your manager copped out then. Look around you. This place is a museum. Not a place to live. Ever see anything like it? The cat who owned this place was a yo-yo. Wait'll you see the rest of it. Go ahead and look."

As if their heads were all fastened to one string, every Partridge head swung to look, as Duke directed.

It was true. All of it.

The upstairs was now utterly dark so that they couldn't see the second floor. But the downstairs of Turnbull House was *something*. Flaring candlelight from the wall niches revealed stone floors, thickly-carpeted. And strange furnishings. A battleaxe hung on one wall, a set of crossed lances on another. A line of battle flags ran along still another wall toward the huge marble staircase. A Union Jack hung side-by-side with the flag of the Original Thirteen Colonies. High overhead, a crystal chandelier dangled like an enormous jewel. There was a heavy-with-dust atmosphere of old age—an unlived-in feeling about the place. Who could say when these walls had last known the sound of family voices?

Shirley got hold of herself. "There are bedrooms, aren't there?"

"About fifteen, all told," Duke said cheerfully. "Take your pick. And there's bedding, too. All the bedrooms are upstairs. Down here's the main dining hall, den, kitchen and study. It's a real cozy place, if you like museums."

"All right. Let's get organized then. I'll get the children into the bedrooms and unpacked. You and I will raid the kitchen to see what we can scrape up. And after that I would appreciate your driving into town to see about all this. There's been a slip somewhere, and I'm sure we can get it all straightened out by morning. Okay?"

Duke grinned. "Okay, Boss Lady."

Shirley shook her head. "Don't call me that. You may call me Shirley."

"Okay!" His smile was genuinely admiring now. "That's beautiful. Just beautiful."

"Now let's get this show on the road," Shirley said, looking at her children.

Danny, arms folded, stared suspiciously at Duke. Christopher was trying to see past his mother's shoulder to the darkened floor above. Tracy had scooped up Simone in her arms to comfort the whimpering little dog.

As for Laurie, she couldn't take her eyes off Duke. Her mother had to nudge her forcibly toward the staircase, telling her to help with the luggage and odds and ends.

Duke, taking the lead, picked up a long yellow candle that had been lying on an old chest and lighted it. Soon the dim glow glimmered up the marble staircase. Its white steps swung upward, and now more shadows came into view.

"This way please," Duke called out. "To your rooms. With hot and cold running water."

Not deceived by his light air, Shirley immediately asked, "Is there really hot water and cold running water?"

"Sure," Duke said over his shoulder. "You have to run down and get it."

Everybody laughed except Danny Partridge.

"Boy," he said grimly, "am I going to talk to Mister Kinkaid about this! He sure let us down—"

The Partridge Family mounted the stairs, following their tall guide. The candlelight wavered and flickered, and each step climbed revealed another niche in the wall, another nook. Rafted beams and great wedge-like timbers now showed, making a vaulted ceiling.

"What is this place called?" Shirley panted, carrying a large suitcase up the stairs directly behind Duke. "Turnbull House? Manor?"

Duke kept on going, without turning around. "Didn't you know?" he called back. "It's Satan Hall."

"*What?*"

"Sure. Satan Hall. You know—Lucifer, the Devil. Fire and brimstone. Seems old Turnbull was a bug for fires. Flames. Red was his favorite color. They put him away years ago. Turn right, now, and follow the leader—"

There was nothing else to do but follow him. He had the candle. Behind and below them, the hall and the staircase were now in deep gloom.

Duke laughed, showing his white teeth in the glare of the candle.

"Well—here're all the rooms. This is what they call the West Wing. You'll find candles all over the place. You all get yourself set and I'll go downstairs and see what gives in the pantry. Okay?"

Shirley immediately began to portion out the bedrooms. There were about ten doors showing in the candle glare, flanking a long, carpeted corridor which ended in a high, badly-splintered window with long drapes sprawling limply to the floor.

As Duke moved off, Laurie's heart moved with him.

The Larkland Rock Festival now promised to be the thrill of her lifetime. Something she could really put in the diary she always kept, no matter what. After all, it was important that she register her ideas and thoughts so that one day she could look back and remember things exactly as they had been. Especially things that were really *relevant*.

Just before Duke disappeared completely from view, Shirley had one more necessary question for him. Laurie joined her at the heavy balustrade as she called down to the young man.

"Oh, Duke—"

"Yeah?"

"Our bus is out on the road. With all our instruments and everything. Any chance of garaging it so it won't be out there all night?"

"Sorry. No garages. I could move the bus though— further off the road."

Shirley sighed. "Never mind then. Guess it can

keep until morning. But I would like to get in touch with Larkland and see what this mix-up is all about."

"Sure thing," he called up. "Right after I fix you something to eat. I'll go in and see what's what—"

"Where's your car?" Shirley asked, suddenly. "Didn't see it when we came in—"

"Bike," he laughed. "I'm a bikeman. It's behind a clump of bush out front. You wouldn't have seen it. A Honda. Greatest set of wheels in the world—"

"Uh—sure," Shirley said, "see you later."

She waved down to him and so did Laurie and then he was gone—swallowed up in the darkness below.

Shirley stood a moment, looking down. When Laurie touched her elbow she almost jumped a foot.

"Oh—! Laurie, don't sneak up on me like that—"

"Mom?"

"If it's about bedrooms, yes, you can have one all by yourself. Keith and Danny will share one and I'll keep Chris and Tracy with me. Now come on, let's get settled down. I've had my quota of disappointments for one day, young lady."

"Okay, but I just wanted to ask you. How old do you think Duke is?"

Shirley almost glared at her oldest daughter, then her expression softened. She shrugged. "Oh, I don't know. Could be anywhere from nineteen to twenty-three. But no more or no less than that. I'd say he's twentyish. Why?"

"Oh, it's just that he seems so alive. So aware of his existence. So relevant—"

"Of course he is, honey," Shirley said, taking Laurie by the elbow. "Now come on and help me with the kids. We'll talk about Mr. Duke later."

Still enchanted, Laurie followed her mother into the nearest bedroom where Keith had two candles flaming and everyone was noisily settling down to life in Turnbull Mansion—or rather, Satan Hall.

Night was coming on, bringing with it deeper blackness, more shadows and more odd happenings. But Shirley Partridge had no inkling of that.

A GOBLIN GIGGLES

☐ Laurie Partridge fidgeted nervously in the big roomy bedroom at the far end of the hall—the one closest to the high narrow cracked window. Mom had let her choose it for herself. She wanted it because its one huge window faced the front of the house and those high iron gates and walls. Keith and Danny were further down the hall in their own bedroom and right next door, Mom was sharing a room with Christopher and Tracy. And Simone. It was close to midnight now but Laurie was far too restless and excited to sleep.

It had been such a wild and wonderful evening.

Duke had served them dinner in a big dining room, complete with high-backed chairs, oval portraits on the stone walls and more brilliant candles shining down from sconces set in brackets. It wasn't any kind of real banquet because all Duke had been able to produce from the kitchen was canned chicken soup, a loaf of sliced bread, and milk. It wasn't much but even Mom had been able to get into the spirit of things and seeing it all as a grand adventure. No phone, no electric lighting, cut off from civilization itself, as it were. Laurie had had no appetite at all. She had been unable to take her eyes off Duke. It was nice to see Mom relaxing and laughing (she always looked so nice when she laughed!) and not worrying about their accommo-

dations and things like that. Duke promised as soon as
the dishes were in the sink, he'd climb aboard the
Honda and go to town to see what was what. And
sure enough, after dinner, with everyone looking at
the books in the old room that looked like a library,
they could hear the put-put-put of his motor racing
away in the night.

After Duke had gone off, Mom had packed them all
up to bed. Keith and Danny had seemed to get on
pretty well with Duke even though he was practically
a *man* compared to them. But Duke had talked to
them as equals about sports, Wall Street, music and
whether or not it was right to fight in Southeast Asia.

Laurie lay awake for a long time in the darkness
straining to catch the returning sounds of the putt-
putt-putting Honda. They never came and she began
to worry, hoping nothing had happened to him. After
all, with the heavy rain all day, and the roads all slip-
pery, it could be very dangerous going into Larkland.

Who *was* Duke? How could such a fine person have
as silly a job as taking care of this old place? Surely, he
wanted something better to do with his life! Like
going into the Peace Corps or running for political
office—Or maybe even going around the world on
only two dollars or something. Any man that looked
as Duke did must do heroic things!

She snuggled into her pillow, eyes closed, with the
house dark and silent all around her.

Then she heard a loose shutter banging on the
ground floor somewhere. The wind must have picked
up. An owl hooted a couple of times, then some crickets or something began to click in the thickets outside.
Overhead, the rafters and eaves of the house all
creaked and groaned. Nothing loud, of course. Just

low, steady, fairly frequent noises. She supposed a person could get used to them after awhile.

Time moved along, slowly, then rapidly. She found herself yawning, her eyes getting heavier. Faintly, from far off, she thought she heard a motorcycle engine but then the sound faded. More silence filled the room. The eaves shuddered, the loose shutter banged again, the crickets started whispering—and she fell into a sound sleep.

By twelve thirty, she was fast asleep.

It would have taken a firecracker to awaken her.

But it wasn't a firecracker that did—it was a terrible sound.

"Hahahhahhhhhhhhaaaaaaaa . . . !"

Laurie Partridge sat bolt upright in bed, blinking against the darkness, every fiber of her being aware of the strange and hideous laughter that sounded as if it were coming from all four sides of the room.

She listened, scarcely daring to breathe, unable to pierce the heavy blackness surrounding her bed. The echoes of the gobbling laugh seemed to linger in her ears. And then, just as she was about to heave a long sigh of relief, it came *again*. Even louder and more terrifying than before.

And *closer*.

"Hahahahhhaaaaaaaaahhaaaaaaa . . .!"

The laughter rolled around the dark room, coming from the walls, the corners, the closets, from beneath the bed, the window. Laurie backed up against the headboard of the bed, pulling the blanket with her, trying to hide. But it was no use. The terrible laughter, so gruesome and un-natural, seemed to grow louder and more insistent until it was the only sound in the universe.

"HAHAHAHAHHHHAAAAAAAAA. . . . !"

Laurie Partridge was as brave as the next girl, but this time she screamed at the top of her lungs—loud enough to wake the dead—*but nobody had come running to see what was the matter!* Not Mom or Keith or Danny or Christopher or Tracy! How could that be? When their rooms were all so close? It just couldn't be! But she hadn't been dreaming. She just hadn't! It was silly to say she had imagined the whole thing—

Or was it?

The mere fact that Mom and the kids hadn't come running was proof enough that she and she alone had heard the terrible laughing. Like a goblin giggling with fiendish delight—

Unless—Mom and the kids *couldn't* come running?

Really terrified now, Laurie bounded out of bed, flew to the door and unlatched it and fled to Mom's room. She banged on the door like a maniac, crying and shouting all at the same time.

She didn't know what she would have done if there had been no answer. But within seconds, the door swept open and Mom was standing there, tousled from sleep, eyes blinking, wondering what was the matter. Her startled expression was something to see.

Laurie Partridge fell into her mother's arms, bawling like a baby.

The frightened barking of Simone echoed from within the bedroom where Christopher and Tracy were now wide awake, and wondering what was the matter.

The first night in Satan Hall was proving to be quite an experience.

While Laurie was sobbing out her wild story about the crazy laughter which no one else seemed to have heard, high up in the shadowy rafters of Satan Hall's attic, a strange scene was taking place.

There, a flickering light of a tall, thick candle sent shadows leaping and bending into the darkness—shadows of the small group circled around the single golden flame.

They sat cross-legged—three boys and two girls, talking in low voices. Candlelight flared on their faces and dimly lighted a stack of blankets and a neat cluster of musical instruments—a banjo, two guitars, bongo drums, and tambourines.

"Man," one of the boys in the group muttered, "I don't dig this scene at all." He tugged a strand of his long yellow hair. "Not at all!"

"I'm with you, Indian," agreed the hollow-cheeked, lank-haired boy sitting next to him. "We'd a-been better off camping out in the open. Mother Nature is alright with me."

"Yeah, Saddle? With all that rain that came down today?" sneered one of the girls.

But the other girl shuddered. "It's just that there's something—*something* about this place. I get a funny feeling. Like—like talking to the dead, you know what I mean?"

The fifth member of the group spoke in a hard voice and his dark eyes flashed. "No, I don't know what you mean. Spell it out, Jenny."

"Well," Jenny hesitated. "Ever feel like you been in a place where you know no one's there, but you'd swear someone's looking over your shoulder? It's creepy. And I'm telling you that's how I feel about *this* place. It's haunted.

"What about it?" asked the yellow-haired boy called Indian.

"When do we split out of here? This place gives me the creeps."

Black eyes snapping, the group's leader spoke. "You cats cool it. When we found this old dump empty, who could have figured there'd be visitors? Man, I dig Larkland the most—and tomorrow I'll be out there in the open country playing my head off, wanting to hear good music. *Our* kind of music. What's the percentage in sleeping outdoors on a night like this? We'll split tomorrow right after that woman and her kids leave."

But yellow-haired Indian still didn't look satisfied. "I still don't like it."

The ringleader's black eyes glared. Nobody ever stood up to him when he looked like that.

"Sorry this isn't the Hilton Hotel," he said in a quiet, deadly voice. "So tomorrow we'll cut out and you cats pick our next stop. Meanwhile, I'm hitting the sack. And we all oughta do the same."

With those words, he reached over to the stack of J. Watterson Turnbull's blankets and began tossing one to each member of the group, then he settled down for the night on the hard attic floor.

Not the miles between Larkland and Satan Hall, but the thickness of a ceiling separated the Partridges from the "caretaker" of Satan Hall.

Duke and his friends slept.

MORE SOUNDS IN THE NIGHT

☐ Laurie would never have had the courage to go back to that awful bedroom if her mother hadn't gone with her. But even with Shirley perched on the edge of the bed, Laurie was still not far from more tears.

"Oh, Mom, am I crazy or something? Hearing things at my age? My ears were checked out okay when Doc Peters gave me my last physical. That was just before we went to—"

"It's all right, honey," Shirley broke in. "Maybe chicken soup and sliced white bread doesn't agree with you. It was a funny kind of supper."

But, Mom! I *heard* it I tell you. Wild nutty laughing. Like a maniac dancing around a bonfire or something—"

"Laurie, stop it. You'll get hysterical again."

"Oh—all right—but I wish you had heard it too. Then you'd know I wasn't dreaming or making any of it up. I couldn't make up that laugh. Not even Boris Karloff ever sounded like that!"

Shirley sighed. It was close to one fifteen now and tomorrow was a big day. She and Laurie needed their beauty sleep. Blast that Duke! Why hadn't he come back?

As though her thought was echoed aloud Laurie asked, "Where is Duke? Why hasn't he come back from town yet? He left hours ago."

50

"I know. I've been puzzling over that too."

"Do you think anything happened to him? Anything bad?"

Shirley smiled. "I doubt that. He looks like a very resourceful young man. In fact, I'd say nothing ever happens to Mr. Duke that he doesn't wish to happen."

Laurie suddenly forgot all her fears and worries.

"You noticed that too, Mom?"

"Noticed what?"

"How cool and groovy he is. Oh, Mom," Laurie laughed self-consciously. "I just think he's the most. Those eyes. That—"

Shirley interrupted. "Right now I'd be more interested in his motorcycle—in hearing it, I mean." She patted Laurie's shoulder.

"And, Laurie—save some of your admiration for Jerry Jingo. You'll be seeing him tomorrow at the Festival, remember."

Laurie blinked. "Jerry who?"

Shirley Partridge laughed. There was no used talking to Laurie about the Festival, now.

"You get some sleep now. I'll be right next door, and if you hear any more laughter, don't scream, just knock on the wall and I'll come running. Fair enough?"

"Fair enough. But I do wish Duke was back."

"So do I." Shirley shrugged. "Chances are he got stuck somewhere and he figures it's too late to come back. So he's waiting until morning."

"He'll be back," Laurie said fervently. "I know he will. He can't come into our lives and walk out just like that. It's Kismet—that means 'fate,' you know. It was meant to be this way."

"It's sleepytime," Shirley yawned. "Hit the sack and stay there. And have pleasant dreams for a change."

"Oh, all right. Good night, Mom. I'm sorry I was such a baby about it—"

"It's no crime to be frightened. Good night, honey."

Alone again, Laurie blew out the candle, then pulled the blankets high, burying her head under the pillow. She intended to take no chances on hearing that dreadful laughter a second time. Huddled under the blankets she soon fell asleep—so soundly asleep that she didn't hear the low-pitched terrible moans that filled the room with horror.

It wasn't diabolical loud laughter this time. It was a faint almost ghostly wailing sound. As of a person in extreme pain or mental anguish.

". . . *oooooooooooooooooo!*"

Then suddenly it changed to a sound even more frightful—the sound of a woman sobbing—great, heart-breaking, anguished sobs.

Laurie Partridge's bedroom tingled with the unknown horror. But blessedly, Laurie slept on. It would have taken a blast of dynamite to awaken Laurie Partridge.

In that strangest room of J. Watterson Turnbull's forsaken manor, the weird succession of sounds went on throughout the dark stretches of the night. The followed a definite pattern. First, the terrible wailing sound like a long hoot of misery. Then the fierce wracking sobs of a woman in great sorrow. And finally a scuffling, clanking noise—as if someone were dragging *chains* across the bedroom floor!

Twenty-four hours before the Partridge family's troubles in J. Watterson Turnbull's strange house had even begun, two widely-separated events were shaping their future. Maybe it was Kismet—fate, as Laurie said.

In New York City, Reuben Kinkaid dictated a telegram to his secretary, Gloria. Gloria was to send it to the Larkland Chamber of Commerce. It would inform them when the Partridge Family would arrive at Mr. Turnbull's deserted mansion in the woods, and that a cook, maid, and chauffeur would be needed during their stay. It also informed them that Reuben Kinkaid, himself, would be arriving to take personal charge of the Partridge Family and that he would put Larkland on the map as the home of the great Rock Festival.

That night Reuben went to bed thinking that Larkland's Rock Festival would make the Partridge Family twice as famous than they already were. They would be twice as much in demand now that rock festivals were all the rage.

Luckily for Reuben's night's sleep, he didn't know Gloria had made a dreadful mistake. The telegram was addressed to Parkland, not Larkland. And Gloria mixed up North and South Carolina, too. It was an awful mistake—the important telegram was sent to the wrong place and wrong state.

And the second event took place far from Reuben Kinkaid's New York City office—in the Blue Rapids Sanitarium. Blue Rapids was a quiet, friendly place—a cluster of low white buildings with attractive green lawns and a fine westerly view of the mountains. But as Reuben Kinkaid was dictating his telegram in New York City, a mild panic was going on in Blue Rapids. For the first time in the history of the sanitarium, one of the patients was missing—none other than old J. Watterson Turnbull.

In the Director's office, a white-jacketed young man with very sad eyes was standing at attention before a glass-topped desk. Behind the desk, the Director, a bald-headed, prune-faced disagreeable man, scowled up at the attendant.

"This is very serious," the Director said as if he was reading a sentence of death in the electric chair. "You know what this means?"

The young man shuffled his feet, looking very unhappy.

"I don't know how it happened, sir. First thing, we were walking in the garden. You know how the azaleas are blooming? He always liked them. Next thing I knew—I had bent down to tie my shoelace—and he was gone! Just like that!"

The Director scowled even more darkly.

"He's a very intelligent and agile man. Considering his years and his case history."

The attendant swallowed nervously.

"He can't get far. The nearest town is twenty miles. He's only wearing his issue sandals. And like you said —he's sixty-five. We ought to flag him down in no time—"

The Director shook his head.

"All these years. Not a black mark against us. And now this. You'd better find him, Williams. Or I'm afraid your days at Blue Rapids are numbered."

"Yes, Sir—ahhh—" The attendant fidgeted.

The Director, watching him, barked.

"Is there something else you haven't told me? Something we ought to know?"

"Ahhhh—" The attendant hesitated.

"Well?"

"Mr. Turnbull does have something in his possession which could—ahhh—make things—slightly difficult."

"Such as?" the Director asked icily, leaning across the desk.

Williams the attendant gulped, almost swallowing his Adam's apple in the process. He looked more unhappy than ever.

"A book of matches," he finally blurted out.

The Director closed his eyes. "No, no, no!" and groaned.

When he opened his eyes again, the attendant was gone. Wisely, he had fled through the office door, obviously not wanting to wait around to explain how J. Watterson Turnbull, a known pyromaniac, had ever been allowed to get his eager hands on a book of matches.

How could he ever explain to the Director that the old guy had stolen the matches from him when he wasn't looking? Weren't the attendants supposed to be smarter than the inmates?

All through that windy night after the rain, rock fans poured into Larkland from all over the United States. They came on motorcycles, in cars, walking, some hitched rides. Some walked. And they all came for the kind of music they loved. It would be a thing of their very own—a musical sit-in to tell the world about love, the milk of human kindness, peace—all wrapped up in a non-violent demonstration of the best that there is, and all the best there *could* be in mankind.

While Shirley and the kids slept and Duke and his followers talked, the hills of Larkland were already alive with the sounds of music, the glow of small campfires—and the good feeling of brotherly love.

It was a beautiful sight to see.

Fifty acres of lovely grassland in the very midst of the Larkland countryside had been set aside for the Rock Festival. And the youth of the nation had responded. Knapsacks, musical instruments, hot dogs, cokes, talk, music, and clustered groups around the campfires—the Larkland Rock Festival was getting underway.

Jerry Jingo, the celebrated movie star, would be flying down by private jet to the airport in the next city. From there he would probably make his approach in his famous all-white Cadillac with the steer-head radiator cap. Beautiful and thrilling Jerry Jingo, star of Music, Screen and Television!

It promised to be the biggest, grandest, most earth-shaking Rock Festival of all.

During those hours before dawn, the owl kept on hooting in trees beyond the house, the crickets chirped and all sorts of insect and animal life stirred within the gloom-shrouded grounds of Satan Hall. J. Watterson Turnbull's house was like some dark gigantic shadow crouched among the trees, down in its circle of damp earth, flanked on all sides by dark forest.

In the house, all slept—the tired Partridge family, and up in the gloomy attic, Duke and his followers. And no one heard the low wail, the dreadful sobs, and the chilling clank of dragging chains.

MORNING AT SATAN HALL

☐ Bright, new, no-doubt-about-it-sunshine was flooding the landscape around the old house when Laurie Partridge awoke in the big bedroom. She felt considerably refreshed, and could hardly believe the terrifying experience of the night before. From her bedroom window, everything looked much better by daylight. The beautiful green grass, the lovely old trees crowding the house, the cobbled walk from the old high iron gates and stone walls, all looked serene, picturesque and pleasing. Laurie almost could convince herself she had imagined the wild laughing. After all, Mom and the rest of the kids hadn't heard it.

Mom poked her head into the bedroom after Laurie answered her call. Mom looked like a million dollars in her red skirt and white blouse. But then she always looked good. Mom had a perfect peaches-and-cream complexion.

"Hurry up dressing, will you, Laurie? You'll have to wash downstairs. The rest of the kids are up already and I want you to give me a hand trying to find some breakfast in that kitchen."

"Sure thing. Any sign of Duke?"

"Not a glimpse. If he doesn't come by ten I think I'll take a run in with the bus. It's ridiculous to stay here and make-do with no real food in the house. And no telephone."

"Check. Be right down."

When her mother had gone, Laurie finished her dressing. She put on a pair of clamdiggers, an open-necked beige jersey and put a pink ribbon in her hair. She would have to wait for a shower in whatever place they'd be staying in Larkland. Right now, all she wanted to do was get out of the bedroom and down to the ground floor where everybody else was. She still hadn't completely gotten over her shaking experience of the night gone by. Hastily, she finished dressing and rushed out of the room.

The corridor, with the cracked high window, letting in a lot of early morning light, was flooded with golden sunshine. A dazzling sight. Not at all the gloomy picture of last night. She paused to watch sun motes spiral down to the wooden floorboards.

And then she heard it—a low, whispery noise.

She recoiled, all her senses alert. Then she realized she was hearing voices. *Boys' and girls' voices.*

And it wasn't anybody in her family!

It was so sudden and startling that she was unable to run. And then she didn't want to. For now, she recognized one of the voices. It was Duke's!

It was Duke who was saying, ". . . split in like ten minutes . . ."

Somebody growled an answer and then there were other voices. Laurie stared around the corridor. Where were those voices coming from? As she walked quietly and quickly along the hall away from the cracked window, the sound grew louder. They were the voices of people who have no fear of being overheard—

"*Dream about any ghosts, Jenny?*"

"*Nah. Guess I was spooking myself—*"

"*Sure you were. Now, let's get our goods and lam*

*out of here—before that family tumbles we're still
here—"*

"*I'm with you, Boo-Boo. . . .*"

Low laughter drowned out the rest of the words but
not before Laurie had found the source of the sound.
A small door, smaller than the bedroom doors, was
slightly ajar as if the wind blowing through the
cracked window at the end of the hall had blown it
open. Laurie held her breath, tip-toed to the door, and
opened it wider. The voices were loud now. She
peered up a long low stairway, hearing the sounds of
scuffling feet and other noises that seemed like people
packing up things. A noise suddenly *plunked* like a
guitar and Duke's voice rose in sudden anger. "*Knock
it off! They can hear that, man!*"

Laurie made up her mind. She *had* to see what was
going on at the top of those stairs. She started up the
steps and the darkened stairway grew lighter the
higher she went. At the top of the steps she stopped
dead.

Duke on the point of slinging an electric guitar over
his wide shoulders turned toward the staircase. His
eyes opened and his jaw dropped.

Indian, on his knees on the dusty attic floor, the
snuffed-out, blackened candle at his side, was looping
the belt buckles of a blanket roll. He looked up, saw
Laurie, and sprang to his feet.

Saddle, his own guitar swinging against his lean,
awkward body halted nervously. And the girls, seeing
her, stared at each other and then back at Laurie Partridge.

"Oh," Laurie stammered, taken aback by seeing
Duke and four strange faces all at once. "I'm sorry. I
didn't mean to interrupt anything—go on with what
you were doing."

That broke the spell. Indian, still on his knees, flung an angry glance at Duke.

"Is she for real?"

Duke settled the guitar over his shoulder. "That's her," he snapped. "And she's real people. You lay off." He turned to Laurie. "Sorry, chick. You just walked in and busted up the party. That changes things. Lots of things."

Laurie shook her head, puzzled. "I really don't know what you mean Duke. You see when you didn't come back last night, we were worried. Mom was, I mean—and now I find you up here in the attic and you don't look like you've been any place like Larkland. Oh, Duke—what is this all about?"

"*Oh, Duke!*" Indian mimicked cruelly, scrambling to his feet. "What are we wasting time for?" He stepped toward her.

Laurie Partridge shrank back against the landing of the attic staircase. Her eyes swung to Duke's for help.

But Duke was shaking his head, almost sorrowfully. "Too bad you had to come nosing in here the way you did. Now, you've spoiled things. We'll just have to take care of you—"

With that, they all closed in on her. Ominously. Quietly.

Duke, Indian, Saddle, and the girls. Like a band of robbers.

Laurie opened her mouth to scream and Duke's hand closed tight over her lips.

"Quiet!" he hissed, and he caught at her flailing arms.

Laurie Partridge closed her eyes. This couldn't be Duke! Her heart pounded. "Oh why didn't I mind my own business and just go down to help Mom with the breakfast as I promised?"

Laurie had a terrible feeling she might never live to know the answer to that one.

She might never *have* breakfast again!

Downstairs, in the big kitchen of Satan Hall, Tracy and Christopher were busily engaged in eating plain white bread with milk. It wasn't much of a breakfast but it was all Shirley could salvage from the food Duke had shown her the night before. Danny and Keith were each grumbling about the plainness of their fare. As for Shirley she longed for a good strong cup of coffee.

Suddenly, as she sat in this huge kitchen of empty cupboards and bare shelves, Shirley realized something was wrong. She clapped a hand to her forehead.

"Laurie!" she said, half-aloud.

Keith looked up. "What about Laurie?"

"She should have been downstairs ten minutes ago. What *is* keeping that girl?" Shirley scowled.

"Probably still mooning over her dream man, Duke. Or Jerry Jingo. I can't keep up with her anymore."

Shirley tried to hide her uneasy feeling of something being wrong. She touched Keith's shoulder. "Go on and hurry her along, will you, Keith?"

"Oh—all right—" Keith pushed away from the table. "I hate to tear myself away from all this good food but—" Laughing, he left the kitchen. Shirley could hear him turning down the hall to the foot of the hall stairs. Then the sound of his steps pounding on the staircase came to them all, below, in the kitchen. Shirley sighed and ordered Tracy to finish her milk. The situation was getting worse all the time. Right after breakfast she meant to hop into the bus and go to town. Keith and Laurie could look after things until she got back—

heir missing member. Somehow, it was a pathetic
and he didn't like looking at it.

Man oh man," he breathed fervently. "They got a
gular dragnet out for her."

"So what do we do?" Indian snarled. "*Now*—I
an."

et's drop her," Duke suggested. "And cut out the
way. Won't matter now. Everybody's out of the
anyhow."

Indian sneered. "You're soft. Knew it all the
We could kidnap this doll and maybe ransom
tfit is big time. We could use the

d you're the one who was wor-
Don't make me laugh. Listen to
p ne says. You're loco."

e it was the short glimpse she had of her
, and Keith, Danny, Christopher, and little
searching the grounds—searching for, worry-
bout her, that turned the trick. But suddenly
wasn't scared. Instead she was angry—right
The handsome Duke and his
aybe Duke kept ugly yellow-
, but he wasn't much different
grubby bunch. Her chin went

tnought, you were real rock people," she said
. "I thought you were *dedicated* to non violence.
nat are you doing going to the Festival anyway?
ou've no business there—you just don't belong to that
erle—either of you!"

"Shut up," Indian gritted and gave her wrist a twist.
urie cried out in pain. Duke whirled from the win-
and pulled her away from Indian's hard grasp.
That does it," Duke said with flat deadly finality.
e came to town to go to a musical sit-in. You make

It seemed no more than five minutes when Keith was back in looking puzled. Shirley's heart sank when she saw his expression.

"Where is your sister?" she asked in a rising voice.

"Beats me. She's not upstairs in her room. Or anywhere on the second floor. I even looked in all the rooms on the ground floor. Maybe she went for a walk around the grounds?"

"But that's ridiculous—she told me she was coming right down. She knew I wanted to get an early start. Are you sure, Keith?"

Shirley was trying to keep the note of hysteria out of her badly-frightened voice. But it was there. She could hear it herself.

"Sure I'm sure, Mom. Would I make it up?"

"Then you couldn't find her?"

"I couldn't find her. Heck, I called her name out so many times, I sounded like a parrot."

"Then where is she?" Shirley Partridge suddenly blurted, the color coming in her smooth face. "*Where could she have gotten to?*"

"Mom," Danny Partridge said very solemnly, getting up from his chair. "Take it easy now. Keith and I are the men in this family. We'll both go and look for her. It's like Keith says. She's probably gone for a walk or something. Don't worry now, will you? Laurie could never get lost and who would ever want to steal her or something?"

Now that Danny had put it into words, genuine terror took over Shirley Partridge. She closed her eyes for a long second, then opened them very calmly and steeling her nerves, spoke quietly. "All right. That's a very good idea. But let's all go and look, yes? It's a lovely morning and maybe the grounds are worth looking at."

She tried not to run as she rallied her family for a search for missing Laurie Partridge. Tracy and Christopher, with Simone tagging along, raced away from the table. Keith and Danny followed, exchanging glances.

Girls were always doing such silly things, weren't they?

But neither of them liked the worried look in their pretty mother's eyes. They never had seen her looking so scared not in all their lives. Not even that time when the bus had blown a tire on the highway when they were on their way to Denver.

It sure was stupid for Laurie to go wandering around like this without telling anybody where she was going—

Women. *Pah!*

In the rear of Satan Hall, where evergreens grew thickly next to barred cellar windows, branches rustled and shuddered, as if something was disturbing them. And something was.

With Shirley in the lead, the Partridge Family had begun on a mass girl-hunt on the grounds surrounding Satan Hall. So no one noticed the stealthy movement in the evergreens where the cellar window was being forced open with the nearest tool available—a handy, rusty old crowbar. The eroded bar of the windows bent easily under the pressure of pudgy thick fingers which for years had tended the gardens and shrubs of Blue Rapids Sanitarium. The newcomer was outlandishly clad in a woolen bathrobe with a corded belt. Scuffed brown sandals protected his feet. A jolly-faced man normally, bent to the task of gaining entry, he looked almost demon-like.

J. Watterson Turnbull owner of
come back home, at last.

In twenty long forgetful years, there
gettable place—the big old house in th
was his. So his running, sandaled feet had
from many miles away—unerringly, witho
so much as a mile off course.

And in his right-hand bathrobe pocket was t
of matches which he had so cleverly stolen fro
silly young attendant, Williams. The idiots! Did
really think he wanted to spend what was left
life tending their silly old gar
foolish azaleas?

No—he had much better thing
At least—*one* better thing.

He'd start another fire—the biggest fire
best one of his flaming career. Why not? It w
the perfect ending to a grand and glorious life
fire-setting.

Certainly, he had every right to burn his own
down.

Who could object to that?

After all, it was his property,

Chuckling to himself, wheez
son Turnbull deftly squeezed
the opened cellar window and lightly
dusty floor of the interior.

His eyes gleamed like a cat's in the darkness.

At the high cracked window outside of Lauri
tridge's bedroom, Duke stared out over the g
Laurie had only one short glimpse of her f
fore she was jerked back from the wind
motioned them all to quiet down. He coul
that the Partridge Family was scouring

It seemed no more than five minutes when Keith was back in looking puzled. Shirley's heart sank when she saw his expression.

"Where is your sister?" she asked in a rising voice.

"Beats me. She's not upstairs in her room. Or anywhere on the second floor. I even looked in all the rooms on the ground floor. Maybe she went for a walk around the grounds?"

"But that's ridiculous—she told me she was coming right down. She knew I wanted to get an early start. Are you sure, Keith?"

Shirley was trying to keep the note of hysteria out of her badly-frightened voice. But it was there. She could hear it herself.

"Sure I'm sure, Mom. Would I make it up?"

"Then you couldn't find her?"

"I couldn't find her. Heck, I called her name out so many times, I sounded like a parrot."

"Then where is she?" Shirley Partridge suddenly blurted, the color coming in her smooth face. "*Where could she have gotten to?*"

"Mom," Danny Partridge said very solemnly, getting up from his chair. "Take it easy now. Keith and I are the men in this family. We'll both go and look for her. It's like Keith says. She's probably gone for a walk or something. Don't worry now, will you? Laurie could never get lost and who would ever want to steal her or something?"

Now that Danny had put it into words, genuine terror took over Shirley Partridge. She closed her eyes for a long second, then opened them very calmly and steeling her nerves, spoke quietly. "All right. That's a very good idea. But let's all go and look, yes? It's a lovely morning and maybe the grounds are worth looking at."

She tried not to run as she rallied her family for a search for missing Laurie Partridge. Tracy and Christopher, with Simone tagging along, raced away from the table. Keith and Danny followed, exchanging glances.

Girls were always doing such silly things, weren't they?

But neither of them liked the worried look in their pretty mother's eyes. They never had seen her looking so scared not in all their lives. Not even that time when the bus had blown a tire on the highway when they were on their way to Denver.

It sure was stupid for Laurie to go wandering around like this without telling anybody where she was going—

Women. *Pah!*

In the rear of Satan Hall, where evergreens grew thickly next to barred cellar windows, branches rustled and shuddered, as if something was disturbing them. And something was.

With Shirley in the lead, the Partridge Family had begun on a mass girl-hunt on the grounds surrounding Satan Hall. So no one noticed the stealthy movement in the evergreens where the cellar window was being forced open with the nearest tool available—a handy, rusty old crowbar. The eroded bar of the windows bent easily under the pressure of pudgy thick fingers which for years had tended the gardens and shrubs of Blue Rapids Sanitarium. The newcomer was outlandishly clad in a woolen bathrobe with a corded belt. Scuffed brown sandals protected his feet. A jolly-faced man normally, bent to the task of gaining entry, he looked almost demon-like.

this chick cry once more and I'm going to lay you out like a rug. Hear me? Now, we let her go and we split out of here. And that's the last word. You dig?"

Before Indian could answer one way or another, Jenny suddenly gasped loudly. She pointed to the high window. "Look!" she whispered hoarsely. "Do you see what I see?"

Just then there was an ear-shattering roar. Whirling rotary propellors of a gleaming silver helicopter buzzed over the grounds of Satan Hall. Like a great mechanical insect the 'copter came whirring over the trees. Then circling and dipping like a pendulum it lowered over a clearing about seventy-five yards off from the house and not far from the high iron gates and stone walls. The toy-like plane settled down in a low vertical landing, giant blades briskly flailing the fine morning air. It shone like a star on the lawn.

Duke and his gang, and Laurie, could see Shirley Partridge and the rest of the kids and Simone racing for the plane.

To the attic intruders the helicopter meant only one thing. Police!

"FUZZ!" Indian shouted. "LET'S SPLIT!"

Everybody did, taking their knapsacks and musical instruments with them. They bounded down the long hall, toward the stairway that led to the ground floor and raced out across the grounds behind the house and to safety.

Left behind was a bewildered and yet relieved Laurie Partridge. Being Laurie, she instantly decided that the 'copter came for one reason—to save the damsel in distress. Herself!

But it wasn't the Law, local or otherwise, arriving in that splendid helicopter.

It was Jerry Jingo himself—the movie star with a *flair*.

THE GREAT JINGO

☐The next fifteen minutes of Laurie Partridge's life were something she would always remember. Everything happened so fast and so furiously that the world seemed to have turned upside down. It was like a wild whirl on a merry-go-round.

For the first moment she could only gaze stupidly after Duke and his pals disappearing rapidly down the hall. Then she went to the window and called down to her mother that she was all right and would be right down. But Mom couldn't hear her because the helicopter was still roaring with its motor wide open, the backwash of the huge rotary blades making the grass flatten back and the closest trees branches bend, bow, and sweep to the grass.

Still shaky and trembling, Laurie hurried down the big staircase, clattered through the baronial hall and rushed out into the open. She ran toward Mom and the kids who were all flocking around the whirly-bird. The engine had now gone silent and she could see a tall man climbing out of the cockpit door.

She would never forget her mother's face when Mom suddenly spotted her. Nor could she have explained the way Mom carried on. Like a baby. Crying, laughing, hugging her until Laurie's ribs ached. It was amazing, really. Even Keith and Danny and Christopher and Tracy joined in the reunion as if they were genuinely glad to see her again. And Simone, barking, wagging her tail, yipped her scruffy head off. In the sudden letdown from tension and nerves, Laurie began to cry too. And that helped Shirley Partridge to pull herself together, brush at her eyes, and demand to know what had happened.

Laurie explained as fast as she could and Mom's eyes got big and round and amazed but before anybody could offer an opinion or a solution, the man who had debarked from the helicopter had ambled over to them waving a hand in a casual salute.

The wonder mounted—*this was no policeman!*

Laurie's eyes almost popped out of her head and memories of Duke fled from her mind. Unless she was seeing things Jerry Jingo in the flesh, was saying hello to everybody and smiling the way he always smiled on the big, wide Cinemascope screen.

Not even out-sized sunglasses, a sloppy blue windbreaker and wrinkled slacks could make Jerry Jingo anything but a dream man.

"Hi," he called breezily to Shirley, the kids, and Simone. "Hope I'm not bustin' up any kind of party."

Shirley shook her head, smiling happily now that Laurie was safe. She extended her hand.

"—we've had a little excitement but it's all over now. And you are Jerry Jingo, of course. We're the Partridge Family."

Jerry Jingo put his hands on his hips and shook his head.

"Well, I'll be blowed. Knew you were coming down here for the Rock show and I kinda thought you all looked familiar." He chuckled good-naturedly. "Shoot! Bet I've got every record you people ever cut. Glad we got a chance to meet like this."

"You're sweet to say that. And I won't tell you how

much the kids and I enjoy your films. And your singing. But what in heaven's name are you doing here? When you drop in, you really drop in, don't you?" Shirley laughed.

He thrust his hands into the windbreaker, tilted his weight on one hip and studied them all. When Laurie realized his eyes, or sunglasses, were focussed on her, she lowered her face, feeling a demoralizing blush flooding her face. But Jerry Jingo didn't seem to notice.

"Fact is, Mrs. Partridge, I didn't expect anyone out here. Heard about this place, being deserted and all, and I was scouting it as a location for my next film. I'd planned to give the place the once-over and call my agent. You see my next flick is going to be about a haunted house in the woods—"

"This must be the place," Shirley said grimly. Then looking toward the helicopter sitting on the grass nice as you please, Shirley smiled. Jingo saw the smile and frowned.

"I say something funny?"

Shirley chuckled. "I thought people under twenty one couldn't get pilot's licenses."

Jerry Jingo laughed. "You got me! I'm really twenty-three, Mrs. Partridge. But you know—show biz. My manager says my image is better if I say I'm about twenty. Dig?"

"Dug." They both laughed and the kids all exchanged startled looks. Twenty-three was pretty old! Then Danny who had been sizing up Jerry Jingo's height, suddenly said out loud. "Six one."

Keith snorted. "Six two and maybe three quarters."

"Six one," Danny insisted.

"What's the difference," Christopher spoke up.

"He's taller than we are. And that makes him tall."

Jerry Jingo, from his great height, said, "Six feet one and a half. Boots always make me look taller."

Laurie had privately estimated that the top of her own head came exactly to the level of Jerry Jingo's firm and chiseled mouth. But the discussion about Jingo's height ended when the young famous movie star wanted to know exactly what sort of excitement he had dropped in on. Shirley hastily explained about the botched arrangements for staying at Satan Hall and Duke's lie about working there when he was really breaking-in and stealing a night's lodging for himself and his friends. At least that was the way she saw the whole thing. Jingo nodded when she had finished and looked almost sympathetic.

"It figures. Some of the kids'll do just about anything to come to something like Larkland."

Keith nodded. "It's going to be something special."

Jingo looked at Laurie Partridge.

"How about you? Feel the same way?"

Laurie nodded quickly and then heard herself saying, "With you and us as a part of it, I don't see how it can miss."

"And have a piece of humble pie," Mom said, and everybody laughed. Laurie really blushed, that time.

"Well," Jerry Jingo said, "How's chances for a look-see around the house? I could use a cup of java too."

"Sorry," Shirley said. "No coffee—no food at all. That's why I have to go into town and see about this—"

Jerry Jingo chuckled. "Got me a whole mess of rations in the plane. Coffee and all. And I'd like nothing better than taking potluck with the Partridges."

Shirley flung her arms around him and gave him a

quick hug. "Just like the movies! You do rescue people in the last reel! You hear that kids? Food! And coffee!"

She led Jerry toward the house while Keith and Danny clambered into the plane to bring out the supplies. Laurie trailed behind. She sighed. Duke *had* been beautiful. But so was Jerry, and somehow the glamor of all his film hits and the magic of Hollywood gave him an *extra* something.

Laurie Partridge's heart bumped. Her diary was going to have an awful lot of fresh entries—the last twenty four hours had given her so much to write about!

It was one of the happiest meals Laurie had ever known. They all ate together in the big kitchen, and simple things like beans, fruit salad, baloney, dark pumpernickel bread, and coffee tasted better than they ever had before.

It was just wonderful to sit with Jerry Jingo and listen to his rich baritone voice and watch his face. With the sunglasses tucked into his windbreaker, Laurie could see that he was even better-looking than he was in the movies. The black curling sideburns, the longish hair, the tanned face, the deep serious blue eyes, the one chin dimple—he was so *groovy*. All in all, Jerry Jingo was a very satisfying reality. Not a disappointment—like Duke.

Danny, the family money expert just had to ask him some financial questions. Danny always tried to learn all he could about contracts.

"How much do you make on a picture, Jerry?"

"Danny!" Shirley protested. "That's none of your business."

"I don't mind," Jerry laughed. "A million dollars

and ten percent of the gross. I'm overpaid, no matter how you look at it."

Danny was so awed by the information he could think of nothing else to say except a mental reminder to discuss *that* with Mister Kinkaid. Christopher had some questions, too.

"Gee. In *Love My Green Beret*, you died real good. I really thought you were a goner, Jerry. How do they do that?"

"Ketchup. Lots of ketchup. And trick photography. The best in the industry."

Tracy clasped her hands together. "I don't like war films. Or westerns. But I did like you in that one about the farm. Where you had to run away from home and then came back a rich man—"

"Thank you, Tracy. Try to do my best. But there's a lot of luck in picture-making—"

Keith Partridge got his two cents worth in.

"How many bikes do you own Jerry? And cars?"

"Five bikes. Three autos. But my favorite machine is a plane—that little bird out there. A real sweetheart."

"Wow!" Keith exclaimed.

Shirley was quietly enjoying the chat her family was having with the famous movie star, when, Laurie suddenly said, "*We're* going to make a picture. Someday. And it will be a big, beautiful thing. With music and romance. Something that will talk to all the kids of the world. You'll see."

"I'll be the first in line for that one, Laurie. No fooling. I'd like to see a picture that's made like that," Jerry said.

"You will," she answered proudly. Her chin tilted. "We've only just got started and already we're way up on all the charts and—"

"Laurie," Shirley said very quietly, "Will you please pass the bread?"

"Sure, Mom."

Jerry Jingo realized Mrs. Partridge really was saying "Let's change the subject." He stood up and stretched his long arms.

"May I see the house now, Mrs. Partridge?"

"You call me Shirley. We've all been calling *you* by your first name. Sure, you can see the house. Laurie, will you—" She halted just in time when she saw Laurie's face.

This was no time to ask a pretty young girl to stay behind and clean up a kitchen—not when a movie star was on the premises! Shirley smiled and spoke to Laurie, "How about your taking Jerry around? You've seen more of this house than we have. We'll clean up down here. And don't be too long, will you? I still have to get to Larkland and straighten out this mix-up, or we'll be sleeping here again tonight."

Jerry Jingo had already sauntered out of the kitchen. Laurie rushed around the table and trapped her mother in a great bear hug. "O, Mom. You're so wonderful!" she whispered.

Tracy, with Simone on her lap, looked up and pouted. "Gee, whiz. I wanted to go too."

Christopher shrugged. "He just wants to look at old rooms. We can talk to him some more later. About more things that are *important*."

"Ten percent of the gross," Danny said, almost goggle-eyed. "You realize how much money that is?"

Keith winced. "Don't remind me."

"Never mind," Shirley Partridge said crisply. "Stop counting the money and start helping me clean up in here. Time's a-wastin' and the Festival begins at sundown tonight. It ought to be beautiful. I don't want to miss that—all those kids and all that good music."

"Shouldn't we be hearing from Mister Kinkaid today, Mom?" Danny asked, still frowning.

"If we don't," Shirley said very grimly, "he will be hearing from us."

"Oh, boy," Keith Partridge said. "I feel sorry for him!"

Simone barked and jumped up and down on Tracy's lap.

Off in the deepest part of the woods, beyond the high walls that surrounded Satan Hall, Duke and the others paused to catch their breath. Their faces were flushed and perspiring, but they were beyond sight of the house now, and no one had followed. And there had been no sign of the helicopter roaring after them. It must have been a false alarm. Maybe that kid, Laurie, hadn't said a word about what had happened.

Duke knew he would have to double back now to pick up his motorcycle, but it was worth the risk. He hadn't come to Larkland to lose a bike that had set him back eight hundred clams. A bike worth twelve hundred on the open market. No, sir.

"Cool it," he told the gang as he sank down on a tree stump. It was exactly then, looking at Saddle and the girls, that he realized Indian was among the missing.

"Hey, man," he blurted at Saddle. "Where's Indian?"

Saddle looked dumb, as he usually did. "Search me. I was just runnin' and not lookin' back—"

Duke climbed off the tree stump, angry now.

"That character—never takes orders—" He flung a

glance at the girls. "Did you see where he got off to?"

They both shook their heads blankly and just as Duke was about to throw a real fit, there was a noise in the brush and Indian came scrambling through. Red-faced, exhausted. But obviously triumphant. He collapsed on the soft grass, leering wickedly. He waved a grimy hand in a feeble salute.

Duke scowled up at him.

"What kept you? Stopping to pick daisies?"

"Lay off," Indian growled. "I was doing what you should have thought of doing, O Great Leader. You're lucky I keep a clear head."

"Meaning just what?"

Indian laughed—a rasping, grating laugh.

"I doubled-back. You know that big old bus of their's? Well, right now, it's just a stone. It can't go any place or even work up a cough. You know what I mean?"

"Talk English," Duke growled. "As much as it hurts you."

Indian shook his head. "I let the gas out of their tank. They couldn't follow us if they tried."

Duke stared at him. He hated to admit it but Indian had made a smart move and one that wouldn't get them into any real trouble. "Well, I gotta go back for my machine," he muttered. "Maybe you and the rest should push on for Larkland."

Indian shook his yellow hair violently. "We'll wait for you. Won't we, gang?"

Jenny and Iris and Saddle all agreed and Indian turned back to Duke and leered. "See, oh Leader? They don't want to leave you. Ain't that sweet?"

For a full moment, the two stared at each other. Duke was first to speak. "Okay. Meet me on the road. Shouldn't take more than ten minutes. But I wish you all had brought your own bikes, like you were supposed to."

"We don't mind walking as long as we can be with you," Indian said, nastily.

Duke started off through the brush again, back in the direction of Satan Hall. He had left his bike hidden in the thickets, just off the roadway, to the left of the entrance gate.

Jenny shivered, as hot as the day was, watching Duke vanish into the brush. "You better stop picking on him. He's just liable to eat you alive and spit you out like watermelon seeds."

"Yeah?" Indian sneered. "That'll be the day."

In his mind, revolt was forming. Some people call it mutiny.

LAURIE'S HEROES

☐ Laurie Partridge was in her glory. Showing Jerry Jingo the house was such fun. He seemed so interested in the old rooms and furniture. Laurie wished she knew enough about their history to be a real guide. No wonder he had so many fans and so many fan letters. He was *really*, a nice person.

With Jerry along, the attic was not so spooky. It almost seemed to Laurie that her awful adventure with Duke and his friends had never even happened—just like that horrible laughter of the night before.

Jerry Jingo seemed very interested in the attic. "Perfect," he breathed fervently. "Just A-1."

"How do you mean, Jerry?"

"Can't you see? Haunted houses have to have attics. Very filmable attics. Look at this one. Skylight. Cracked glass. Cobwebs. All those corners and nooks. And dig this floor. Ready to splinter and creak and groan. Yeah. The scene is kinda just right."

While Jerry and Laurie talked in the attic, down at the bottom of the attic steps, a cherubic old man in a bathrobe and sandals, crouched listening. The book of matches was held poised in his chubby fingers. The little eyes in the jolly face were screwed up with great intensity, as if he was trying to make up his mind about several things.

Who were these strangers in his house? Should he

wait until the people were gone then start an attic fire? Or should he pick another spot to get things burning?

J. Watterson Turnbull heaved a low sigh. The worst thing about being away from Blue Rapids was having to think for himself. Decisions were never very easy— at least, not for J. Watterson Turnbull. So he squatted at the foot of the stairs, eavesdropping, as Jerry Jingo and Laurie Partridge talked.

Finally the talking ended and footsteps approached the top of the staircase. The old man scuttled back the way he had come—across the hall and into one of the bedrooms on the other side of the corridor.

"What was that noise?" Laurie asked sharply.

"Didn't hear anything," Jerry Jingo said.

Laurie sighed. "Must be me. Oh, well. Haunted houses just aren't for me I guess."

And yet Satan Hall did have a certain sort of charm, Laurie thought. Especially when a movie star was in the vicinity!

Duke had reached the place where his bike was parked. It was only a short distance from the big Partridge Family bus.

He approached cautiously, eyes peeled for any observers on the scene. There weren't any. He stalked toward the hiding place and began to part the brambles and leaves covering the Honda. He had barely started when the sound of a car motor made him jump. Quickly, he ducked into a thicket—and none too soon!

A blue convertible, top down, was cruising up to the high iron gates of Satan Hall. A worried-faced blonde man behind the wheel. He was looking anxiously at the iron gates as he cut the motor. Then he scrambled out, very stiffly, straightened his orange tie, and reached into the car for a black leather attache case.

It was Mr. Reuben Kinkaid, coming finally to the rescue of the Partridge Family.

Duke waited until the stranger had squeezed through between the bars of the iron gates. Then he decided that whatever Indian could do, he could do better!

He stole out of the bush and warily approached the blue car. Grinning, he went around to the gasoline tank. It wasn't long before gas began trickling to the ground.

As an added clincher, he let the air out of the tires.

Then he wheeled his bike out of the brush, and onto the road. He climbed aboard, revved the engine and the bike shot forward, *putt-putt-putted*, blasting the silence, and zooming into action. In a moment, Duke was far down the road, leaving only shattered silence behind.

Laurie and Jerry Jingo had reached the main staircase when Laurie heard the roar of the motorcycle. For one crazy second, she thought that Duke was coming back—to tell her that he was sorry, that he would reform and that he owed all his change of character to her.

"You heard something again, Laurie?" Jerry asked.

"Yes. That bike. Hear it?"

"That I do. Sounds like a bad muffler to me."

Laurie sighed. The sound of the bike had faded into nothingness. "I wouldn't know anything about that," she admitted. "That boy, Duke, Mom spoke about—he said he had a bike."

"I get it. You liked him?"

"Oh, kind of, at first." She frowned. "You can tell a lot by looking at a person's eyes, don't you think?"

"Come on," Jerry laughed. He took her arm and steered her in the direction of the kitchen.

Laurie followed and was amazed to hear a very very familiar voice issuing from the big kitchen.

"Shirley, I give you my blessed word I had no idea you were all down here without the local officials knowing anything about it! I'm going to fire that numbskull secretary when I get back to New York—"

"Don't do that, Reuben," Mom was saying in a very clear, very sweet voice. "Just get me a maid, a chauffeur, a cook. Hot and cold running water. Electricity. Stuff like that."

"Yeah," Danny was chiming in. "If the press ever gets word of this, Mister Kinkaid, it'll destroy our image—"

Laurie grinned. She knew that the good ship Partridge Family was back on even keel and in safe harbor once more. Nothing could go wrong now— not with Reuben Kinkaid in charge.

At least, she didn't think so.

But upstairs in the old house, the odd figure in bathrobe and sandals was very busy. J. Watterson Turnbull had found just the place to start his fire! He had set his sights on the main bedroom—the one he himself had slept in for so many years before those men in the white uniforms had come to take him away so long ago he couldn't remember exactly when.

It was a big room and the feather ticking in the old pillows on the big bed and those lovely moth-eaten drapes, would make excellent fuel for his book of matches. What a blaze they would make! A conflagration!

J. Watterson Turnbull knew all about how to start a fire. He was an expert and it didn't take him long either.

The little matches tongued the drapes and soon a merry series of little fires were burning all over the big room. The old man stood in the center of things, watching his handiwork take hold. Oh, it was going to be beautiful, all right. He could tell!

Orange flame licked up the length of the drapes, touched the gause-like curtains and they billowed out magically in flames. Old paint and varnish fed the fire. Now, the room was alive with lovely, blazing flame. Red, orange and magical. The old man rubbed his hands together happily, and watched it all.

Soon the entire room would be one great, grand and glorious blaze.

J. Watterson Turnbull began to dance around the room. Like a mad Rumpelstiltskin, rubbing his hands, and chuckling loudly. Soon he began a wild and singing chant of glee.

> *"For tonight I'll merry merry be . . .*
> *Merry merry be . . . merry merry be . . .*
> *For tonight I'll merry merry be . . .*
> *Tomorrow I'll be sober . . . !"*

The bursting flames seemed to dance in time to his words. And all about the big room, a very dangerous, hazardous fire now leaped and crackled.

A HOUSE IS NOT A BONFIRE

☐ Out on the fifty sloping acres allotted by Larkland for the Rock Music Festival, rock fans had become a human tide. The land was filling to the brim. People, young people, all sizes, shapes, ages and colors streamed over the countryside.

Late afternoon sun glittered on beards and love beads, and on musical instruments everywhere. It glowed on flowered garb and even more exotic costumes of the hundreds in that huge mass of people.

Tents had sprung up, campfires were kindled and sleepy-eyed *gurus* were calling for demonstrations of peace, love and affection.

Television cable trucks and cameramen were trying to interview the participants. Entertainers too had arrived. Groups like *The Elephant Five, Sandy and Sonny and Sid, The Apes, The Loving Six* and others. A mammoth makeshift wooden stage had been built at the far end of the long green slope. Microphones and amplifiers had been rigged so that even if fifty thousand people showed up, nobody would miss anything —not so much as a clinker.

Cooler weather was promised for sundown. What everybody would eat and how they would cook was something left largely to guesswork. And maybe, good luck.

Larkland was getting ready for its Rock Festival.

No matter what happened, many of the performers felt, this would be a great musical sit-in. It would be the music of soul and spirit—music of a generation that wanted the end of wars everywhere and sang its message of love and peace.

Shirley Partridge had steered Reuben Kinkaid, Jerry Jingo and her family to the immense main room of Satan Hall. It was a place where they could all talk comfortably around the long oaken table. Reuben was more than glad that Jerry Jingo had "dropped in." He knew the publicity value would be sensational. And after what had happened to Shirley and the kids so far, they deserved a break like this. From what he'd already been told, they'd certainly had had a rough night and morning. When he thought about what *could* have happened, he broke into a cold sweat.

But everything was groovy now—real groovy, as the kids might say! But what were managers for—if not to worry? Danny Partridge, as usual, kept hounding him. "How's Wall Street, Mister Kinkaid?" Kinkaid winked at Jerry Jingo to let him in on the joke and said very seriously, "Awful. U.S. Steel dipped three points, Coca-Cola is up five and Mrs. Wagner's Pies made a resounding come-back, jumping twenty points in one hour on the Floor."

Everybody but Danny laughed. He looked very dignified. "Just because I'm interested in what's happening to the financial state of the nation is no reason for levity, Mister Kinkaid," he said, using his larger words.

Reuben immediately apologized, knowing how sensitive the young redhead was. "You're right, kid. But don't worry. Your financial state is very good. That's all you need to worry about. Number One. Always look out for him."

Jerry Jingo nodded his head. "That's a fact. Only trouble is—in Shirley's case, she has to look out for Numbers One, Two, Three, Four, and Five."

That got a laugh too but Keith loyally responded to the kind-hearted jibe. "Mom does okay in that department."

"You bet," Tracy and Christopher chorused.

Shirley smiled. "Thank you one and all. But let's talk about the Festival. I am excited about that. All those young people coming from miles away just to do their own thing." She shook her head, visibly awed. "Hard to beat a scene like that."

Jerry Jingo nodded and smiled.

"That's what it's all about, Shirley. Doing your own thing. Guess it's what we all want when we get down to the nitty-gritty. What do you say, Laurie?"

Laurie looked around the big table. Everybody was looking at her, especially Mom. With that funny proud affectionate look in her eyes again.

"Yes," Laurie said very carefully and clearly. "I think it's such a beautiful expression of the youth of this country. And such a beautiful way of showing how they feel about things. I think it's a privilege and an honor that we were all invited the way we were."

"Hear, hear," Reuben Kinkaid pounded the table with his hand.

Simone barked noisily until Tracy shushed her up.

Jerry Jingo smiled at Laurie.

Laurie lowered her eyes under that smile, but she could feel her knees trembling with joy and happiness.

Shirley clapped softly. Her eyes shone. "I agree. Now, shall we all decide, children, what the Partridge Family is going to play this afternoon and this evening? I have a fair idea all our standards would be a good beginning but I am open to any suggestions—"

Keith snapped his fingers. "Maybe it's a good time to introduce *My Hands Were Made For You?*"

Reuben Kinkaid shook his head vehemently.

"No dice. You play that and Arco Records will blow their tops and our contract. They want to send that out next month with a big surprise introduction. Pick something else, please. Now I'm glad I did come out here. You people are dangerous—don't you read your contracts? Arco has a genuine exclusive on that number."

"Sorry," Keith said sheepishly, "I forgot." Suddenly his expression changed. "Hey—what's that funny sound?" Everybody listened. It was true. There was a dull, faraway, roaring noise.

"Probably a plane," Shirley said. She shrugged. "Well, back to business. Suppose we open up with the act we did in Nevada? The curtain goes up, you're all sitting on stools—though maybe they might not have any in Larkland—and I introduce you—. What's the matter, Reuben?"

Reuben Kinkaid of all people was wrinkling up his nose. Reuben usually said what he meant, but Shirley had never seen him show disapproval in that way.

She frowned, her feelings hurt. "Did I say something wrong, Reuben?"

He blinked at her, then sniffed again. "No, of course not—but did you leave something burning in the kitchen?"

She grinned, relieved.

"Not a chance. No cooking, remember? We ate cold food."

He shook his head.

"Then why do I smell something burning—?"

It was a crazy question and Simone was the first to give an answer. She suddenly let out a series of frightened yips and raced under the table. The kids and Jerry Jingo all rose instantly. Nobody had been smoking a cigarette. Not even Reuben Kinkaid. But in a swift and terrible instant, everybody had the answer—an ugly answer.

"Jeepers!" Danny yelled. "Look!"

They all looked.

Curling into the big room from the hall was a long, black tongue of smoke. It snaked and curved toward them as they stared in horror.

J. Watterson Turnbull's most glorious fire had finally sent its first feelers to the floor below.

Upstairs, Satan Hall was already roaring in flames. The savage, deadly roar could be heard by everybody.

It hadn't been a plane at all—Satan Hall was on fire!

Laurie Partridge shrieked like the frightened damsel in distress she had *really* become.

"Hey, give a look at that!" Duke, who had rejoined his group, pointed toward the sunny sky. Rising like a smoke signal was a dark cloudy column. It came from the direction of Satan Hall. As they stared, the smoke began to billow, thicken and fill the horizon above the level of trees.

"Gee," Jenny said, "You think it's a fire?"

"Sure," Iris offered, scratching her elbow. "Somebody's probably burning leaves."

"In the middle of summer?" Duke murmured. "Not a chance."

"So what?" Indian growled impatiently. "Let's split."

"They could be in trouble back there," Duke said quietly. "And maybe it's all that gasoline you spilled,

Indian." He hadn't yet mentioned what he had done to Reuben Kinkaid's blue convertible.

Saddle shrugged. "If it is a fire then maybe we'd better vamoose. They'd blame us first thing. C'mon. I'm moving."

Duke suddenly made up his mind.

"I'm going back. I don't like it. That old house catches fire and it'll burn down half the woods—"

"Are you nuts?" Indian snarled.

"Shut up," Duke said, remounting his motorcycle. "I'm going back. You all do what you want to do. I'll see you in Larkland."

Indian turned to the rest of the group. He leered triumphantly.

"See? What did I tell you? You can't rely on him in a tight squeeze. There he goes running off again. Well, I'm going to Larkland. If the rest of you smarten up, you'll do the same!"

Duke didn't bother to answer, nor to wait for their decision. He zoomed off in a blasting racket of noise and disappeared in an instant.

The main room of Satan Hall was suddenly pandemonium.

Everybody was rushing around, shouting, yelling, trying to make some sense out of what was happening. It was difficult to do. Simone barking furiously, her nostrils irritated by the black smoke streaming into the big room, didn't help a bit.

Fortunately, Jerry Jingo and Reuben Kinkaid did not lose their heads. The hallway was quickly beginning to fill with choking, acrid black smoke, and they could see that the crawling, creeping tongues of orange and red flame had started to eat their way down the stairs.

Reuben Kinkaid and Jerry Jingo were equal to the task of keeping a panic from spreading. Rapidly, Jerry commanded the kids to lock hands together and he grabbed Laurie Partridge's fingers. Reuben snatched Shirley Partridge and in quick formation, the entire group stumbled through the smoking darkness toward the big front door. Shirley choking and gasping behind Reuben, wondered for a brief terrified instant how so many bad things could happen to her family, all in a day and a half.

But there was no time for anything but action. They had to get out of the house before it burned down around their ears.

They coughed and gagged and the heat of the hallway was now intense. Reuben Kinkaid cried out in pain as his bare hand brushed against the suit of armor standing by the front door. Its metal surface was burning hot. Jerry Jingo called for order, and they finally made it to the front door. Keith hung onto Danny, Danny to Christopher and Christopher to Tracy.

Behind them all, Simone was still barking furiously.

"Simone!" Tracy suddenly screamed. "Simone's still back there!"

Laurie Partridge didn't think twice. She broke from Jerry Jingo's strong grasp, and darted back through the smoke to the entranceway of the main room, and there was Simone, too frightened to go farther. *"Laurie!"* Jerry yelled. *"You come back here!"* He strained to see her in the now blinding smoke.

Laurie scooped up Simone's scruffy, trembling body, and plunged back through the smoke, to the others.

At the front door, Jerry Jingo grabbed the heavy handles and jerked back with all his strength. It did not swing open. It was closed so tight that Jerry's

strongest efforts could not budge it. Sweatfaced,
amazed, he looked back. It was too late to duck to
make a run for the back door. They'd never get
through that smoke and flame, rising, choking, awful.
There was no way to turn. Shirley, Reuben Kinkaid,
and the children crowded fearfully against him, trying
to press away from the smoking horror that Satan Hall
had become.

"Jerry—" Shirley cried frantically, trying to see
through the smoke. "What's the matter with the door?
Are the bolts swung back?"

Jerry couldn't tell her what he suspected. "Stand
back! Give me room!" He hurled his full one hundred
and eighty-five pounds at the unyielding door, and his
heart sank. He faced the truth.

They were locked in a house that was burning
down—in a house *locked from the outside!*

J. Watterson Turnbull had left the burning master
bedroom long before this. As he skipped happily and
swiftly down the main staircase and out the big oak
doors there was only one thought in his simple head—
the beautiful sight he'd soon be watching from the
front lawn.

Carefully he had closed the door behind him. Then
reaching up to the heavy brass-monkey door knocker,
he had given it a sharp turn, first left, then right. Then
he tried the door handle. Locked! He beamed with
satisfaction. His very own burglar-proof invention was
working as well as it had years and years ago.

If J. Watterson Turnbull had heard any people talking in his kitchen he would have demanded that they
leave. It was *his* house, wasn't it? Why should those
people have been in *his* attic? Well, nobody would

ever come in again! He'd locked the door!

He trotted across the lawn to get the best view possible. All he ever wanted out of life was a good roaring fire—and he certainly had one now! Billows of black smoke poured from the upstairs window. Soon he'd see his beloved scarlet flames!

DUKE TO THE RESCUE

☐ Duke, driving fast, reached the gates of Satan Hall in no time at all. There was no need now to wonder if he had done the right thing. Thick, billowing smoke proved it. Satan Hall was on fire. There was a choking, cindery, dusty feel to the air.

Quickly, Duke skidded his bike to a stop, flung off the saddle, and clambered through the opening in the gates. Within seconds, he was rushing down the narrow lane to the flaming mansion. Its upper half nearly hidden by roaring smoke and flame, and the air was filled with hideous, crackling.

Duke raced down into the center of the property. In one quick flash, he took in the frightening scene.

He saw the big silvery helicopter poised on the lawn far from the house. It look like a strange bird.

And he saw a weird figure clad in bathrobe and sandals, dancing and skipping on the lawn about twenty yards from the house. But where was the Partridge family?

He did not stop to think twice. He bounded across the lawn to the big front door with the brass monkey doorknocker. Now, even with the smoke and crackling sounds of flame, he could hear the thumping sounds from the other side of the door. People were trapped inside the house—and it didn't matter who they were.

Grimly, his eyes slitted against the smoke, Duke threw himself at the door. He fumbled with the handles, twisting and turning them rapidly. Nothing happened. Desperately he grabbed the brass-monkey doorknocker and twisted it left and right, as he pressed the handle with his other hand. Instantly, the snap-lock released and the door swung inward. Duke lurched forward then stepped back—not a second too soon.

A mass of humanity spilled on by him. Jerry Jingo, face blackened, Shirley Partridge, grimy and sooty, and all the kids. Laurie Partridge stumbled past him, lurching and staggering away from the burning house toward the safety of the wide lawn. Then Reuben Kinkaid came barreling on through the door, head down, and still hanging onto his precious attache case.

As black smoke gushed through the open entrance, Duke slammed the door shut then ran for dear life. It was not a moment too soon. A splintering, flaming slat of oak crashed down from the archway, exploding into fiery cinders. The twin marble columns of Satan Hall were no longer white.

Out on the lawn, everybody had slumped to the grass, gasping for life-giving air. Simone lay on her side, whimpering again. Laurie gazed at Duke and in spite of her smarting eyes and throat, the biggest smile in the world lit up her face.

"You came back—you came back!—and I knew you would—" she cried.

Danny and Keith grinned, and Shirley Partridge stood up and gave him a grateful hug. Christopher and Tracy were, for once, not saying a word. Jerry Jingo flung out his right hand and pressed Duke's.

"Nice goin', pardner. You sure pulled our fat out of the fire."

Not to be outdone, Reuben Kinkaid stammered, "Young man, they should cast your statue in deathless bronze! If you hadn't come along, when you did—"

Duke cut in, "What happened?" he asked Laurie.

But Laurie was staring across the lawn. The weird old man was still prancing and waving his arms toward the house. "Who is *that?*" she exclaimed.

"Don't know," Duke said, grimly, "but I'll find out."

Jerry Jingo glanced at the fiery furnace Satan Hall had become, then turned to look at his helicopter. "Make it fast, boy. We still got to get out of here. That building is going to touch off everything within a thousand yards of this place. And I got to get that whirly-bird up, up and away."

Christopher and Tracy still were looking pretty badly frightened. Shirley hugged them to her, her eyes filling with tears. She was still too grateful to say much of anything. Duke didn't wait but walked quickly. Swiftly Duke, Jerry, and Reuben Kinkaid strode over to the old man. Reuben was beginning to put two and two together and didn't like what he was adding up.

"Hey, old man—" Duke tugged at the old man's sleeve. "Don't you think you ought to stand back?"

J. Watterson Turnbull spun around and faced the three men, eyes filled with tears.

"I didn't know there were people inside!" His voice shook. "I *never* want anybody to get hurt!"

The men exchanged glances. Reuben Kinkaid coughed, then spoke gently. "Who are you?" he asked.

But the old man shook his head back and forth. "Fires are so pretty, aren't they? And that's a good one, isn't it? One of my very best. But I never would have set it off if I knew that people were in the house —and such a nice dog, too. I don't understand it at all. It's *my* house!"

"You mean you *started* the fire?" Reuben asked quietly.

"Of course." The old man brushed at his eyes. "It's my hobby. And after all, I was only burning down what's mine. Satan Hall always had it in her to make a good fire. I knew it. I just knew it!"

More fiery cinders and crashing beams sounded from the blazing house before them. Jerry Jingo turned impatiently, toward his shining plane. Another ten minutes and there was no telling if he'd be able to take off. "Come on," he urged. "We can talk later. Let's get out of here—"

"Wait a second," Reuben Kinkaid argued. "This is very important, Jingo. I have every reason to believe this is J. Watterson Turnbull, the owner of that house—"

"You know my name," J. Watterson Turnbull crowed. "That's nice. Heard of me, have you? Was it the Larkland factory fire or the one I set in the old amusement park after they closed it down?"

Kinkaid took the old man's arm and motioned Duke to take the other.

"Yes, Mr. Turnbull. Everybody's heard of you. And now if you'll come with us, I'll give you a ride in my nice blue car back to Blue Rapids." He winked at Jerry Jingo to lead the way. Jerry needed no urging. But Duke looked down at his boots. "Sorry, chief," he said to Reuben. "Your car has no gas in it and no air in the tires. I'll explain later."

"What do you mean?" Kinkaid exploded. Duke shook his head. There was no time now for explanations. Hurriedly the three men led J. Watterson Turnbull back to Shirley and the kids. Then they all started toward the front gates of the property. Behind them, the house was a bonfire now. Red angry flames were shooting up toward the sky, casting a blackening pall over the yellow sun.

From far off came the shrieking, piercing sound of a siren. It was keening like a banshee and the air was alive with the sound. "Larkland Fire Department," Duke laughed, harshly. "Just in time to water down the ashes."

"This is kind of a deserted neighborhood out here. Be glad they come at all," Jerry snapped.

Shirley nodded. "Let's get in the bus and wait for them. If the fire gets too close, I can always pull out."

Duke started to speak, then stopped.

J. Watterson Turnbull kept casting anxious glances back at his great fire.

But his old eyes glittered with pride and happiness. The children kept stealing furtive glances at him. They had never met such a strange old man. Tracy especially couldn't take her eyes off him.

Jerry Jingo paused at the gates.

"This is as far as I go. Gotta get the chopper out of there or I lose about twenty thousand bucks worth of airplane. See you all at Larkland and this has been some weenie roast, let me tell you."

Laurie looked up at him. He too had been a real hero through the whole affair. He smiled down at her and then bent hurriedly to peck her on the cheek. Shirley shook his hand warmly and he kissed her too. Then Jingo looked at Duke and raised his hand in a salute—the Peace gesture.

"You be there too. Hear? I'm going to get you a part in my next picture. 'Bye all. Gotta run."

With that, he dashed back into the grounds. They

all smiled at one another and Duke blinked foolishly. His mouth worked.

"Hey, is that really who I thought it was? Jerry Jingo? Figured he looked like him but I never for a moment believed it."

"That's him," Laurie said proudly. "And wasn't that sweet of him?"

Reuben Kinkaid angry about his car, was in no mood for conversation. "Let's get out to the bus," he said, harshly. "Those fire engines ought to be here any minute. This way, Mr. Turnbull."

"Why thank you, young man."

They all clustered beyond the walls outside the Turnbull property and headed quickly toward the big bus down the roadway. Laurie smiled up at Duke. Her faith in mankind, and Duke particularly, was restored.

Even on the road, the smell of smoke and fire was overpowering. There was an acrid, biting tang to the atmosphere. Dusty cinders sailed over the high walls. Random sparks flew through the air. Then the crackling noisy air was bombarded by the blasting roar of the helicopter. Soon they saw it, rising like an elevator over the earth. Jerry Jingo banked the plane sharply overhead, and dipped down to wave goodbye from the cockpit window. Then the plane rose again and shot off toward the direction of town. Everybody waved back and the kids clapped their hands in approval. And relief.

The siren sounds now grew louder, too. Drawing closer all the time.

They crowded into the bus and Reuben Kinkaid steered J. Watterson Turnbull to a seat, then sat down across the aisle so he could keep an eye on him. In Reuben's estimate, the old man was harmless enough without matches in his hand. He would turn him over to the authorities as soon as was possible. But he broke out into a cold sweat when he thought what had nearly happened. If this Duke what's-his-name hadn't come along like the Seventh Cavalry arriving in the nick of time. *Phew!* A kid on a Honda!

Laurie and Duke sat together in the middle of the bus.

"You came back," Laurie said softly not looking at him.

"I had to."

"I knew you would."

"How did you know?"

"I just knew that's all."

"Knew what?"

"That you weren't like your friends."

"He's no friend of mine," Duke sighed. "Just a born troublemaker. Never should have let him come along to the Festival with us."

Laurie looked at him then, shyly, then started to speak.

"Which one is your girl? Jenny?"

He shook his head. "Neither. No, man. I don't dig that scene."

"Too bad."

He turned to stare at her. "Why is it too bad?"

"Because," Laurie said quite distinctly but in a very low voice so that her mother and all the rest couldn't hear her. "I think . . ."

But she never completed her sentence. Just then J. Watterson Turnbull started to cry hard. The sobs were so sudden and startling that everyone in the bus jumped. Reuben Kinkaid jumped and leaned over him. "Here now, old timer, what's the matter?"

"My house. My beautiful house," J. Watterson Turnbull cried.

"You'll build another one," Kinkaid soothed him.

"It's not that, it's all that beautiful machinery. All my tricks. And inventions. I shall miss them now. Never to hear them again—"

Shirley Partridge who hadn't yet settled herself behind the wheel, perked up her ears and looked at Laurie. She asked very gently, "Tell us about them, Mr. Turnbull. Sounds like fun. I'm sure the children would like to hear about it, too. Wouldn't you, kids?"

Danny, Keith, Tracy and Christopher all nodded eagerly. Laurie sat up and paid close attention. Mom suspected something, Laurie was sure of that.

"Really? You think so?" Magically, J. Watterson Turnbull beamed, his tears all gone as quickly as they had come. "Oh, my, yes. It was a wonderful house, that place. The bedrooms had all sorts of things in them. For fun, you see. I used to like to scare people who came to see me. Especially the bedroom at the end of the hall. My favorite room. With the laughing man, the crying woman, and the chains. Ah, a masterpiece. My own invention, too." He sighed happily.

Shirley persisted. "Go on. Tell us about it."

The old man wagged a finger at them. His tiny eyes gleamed.

"Well, I sound-proofed that room. Nobody outside could hear a thing. About an hour after a person lay down on the bed, a thin panel in the wall slid back and the sounds would begin. Then after another hour it would start again. I had the sound of a woman crying, a man laughing and the dragging of chains across the floor. And it could work four times before it stopped." He smiled. "It was my own invention. It worked by a secret mechanism which I will not reveal. I suppose it could drive a person out of his mind, at that—" The smile vanished from his face and he looked tearful again. "But it's gone now, isn't it? All gone. My beautiful house and I'll have to go back to that silly old Blue Rapids and take care of those silly azaleas again. Oh—why did I burn my house down . . . ?"

Kinkaid sighed helplessly and Shirley looked at Laurie. Their eyes confirmed what they both now realized. Laurie had spent the night in J. Watterson Turnbull's special room—complete with Laughing Man, Sobbing Woman and Dragging Chains. Though Laurie had slept soundly through the sound of sobs and chains, at least she now knew she hadn't imagined the horrible laughter. And that was a relief to know.

Shirley walked away from the old man who had quieted down and sat down in the driver's seat. She had decided it was high time to leave. She was dismayed when the bus tried to groan into life but then didn't budge. A quick look at the gasoline gauge surprised her. Why, she had filled the tank only twenty miles from Satan Hall.

"That's funny," she blurted. "We seem to be out of gas—" Duke cleared his throat, unhappily.

"Ahhh, I think I'd better explain about that, Mrs. Partridge. You see—"

Reuben Kinkaid favored him with a steady glare from across the aisle. Duke began to explain, but the air was suddenly filled with the siren whine of a red fire engine and a special car racing down the roadway toward them and Satan Hall. The Larkland Fire Department had arrived at last—too late to save the house, the way it finally worked out. But in time to take everybody back to town and take J. Watterson Turnbull to the police and a nervously-waiting Williams, the attendant hot on the trail of his missing patient.

In Larkland, the yellow sun dipped beyond the range of blue-green hills. A soft cool breeze washed over the panorama of waiting people. The Larkland Rock Festival was about to start.

ROCK TIME IN LARKLAND

☐ "Mom?"

"Yes, Laurie?"

"Oh, come on. You know what I'm talking about."

"No, I do not, Laurie Partridge. And I wish you'd stop posing riddles when we're trying to get ready to do a show."

The Partridge family was gathered on the tip of the fifty acres of Larkland dedicated to the Festival. A sea of faces was visible as far as the eye could see. And the Partridges, ready in their matching costumes of open vests, ruffled shirts were nervously pawing the dusty ground like excited show horses. They'd played before huge crowds before, tough crowds, but nothing could be tougher than this. Their real audience—that had created them. Here were the young people who had made the Partridge Family and its kind of music their thing. Shirley wanted the kids to be nothing short of great and here was Laurie, stopping in the middle of nowhere to ask a silly question!

Up on the makeshift wooden stage *The Loving Six*, half a dozen of the best young rock singers in creation, were blasting the skies with their own incredible rendition of *Worry Me, Baby*. The air was throbbing with the impact of thousands of young souls responding to the four-beat beat. It was a sound of

tting

lead seri-

be about

to Dad very
e been more than

go to sleep now?"
s for the talk."
And good night, honey."

beauty and superior musicianship—a tough act to follow.

"Come on, Mom," Laurie pleaded, looking lovely in her costume. "Jerry Jingo or Duke. Who do you like best?"

"For heaven's sake," Shirley wailed, helping steer a ribbon through little Tracy's hair while Keith, Danny and Christopher stared goggle-eyed up at the great stage where *The Loving Six* was weaving its own brand of rock magic. "What a question to ask!"

"Well. Which?"

"Laurie Partridge, honestly! Listen, you think about our first number and just forget about those two for an hour at least. Okay?"

"All right, Mom. But it'll be hard. How do I look?"

"Just perfect, honey. What about me?"

"Not bad at all for a woman with five children, I should say."

They both laughed and the tension snapped. Little Tracy was busy, silently mouthing her lyrics the way she always did before they went on. Keith was adjusting the strings of his guitar and Christopher was lightly patting his drums. Danny was busy, too, trying to estimate the crowd, and figuring that if each person had had to pay a dollar how much . . . ? But there was no charge, none at all. This one was on everybody. And everybody was out there—looking on, cheering, having fun, making music and larking under the stars. Even Reuben Kinkaid was on the edge of the crowd, making certain that the TV cameramen and the rest of the newspaperman mob were doing their job the way they were supposed to. They were. Flashbulbs were popping all over the place and the TV monitors were moving continuously over the scene.

Reuben was happy. The Partridge Family was alive

and well and in Larkland—rescued from a burning house and no more Satan Hall for the Partridges. The Chamber of Commerce had arranged rooms for them right in the center of Larkland.

And J. Watterson Turnbull was safely on his way back to Blue Rapids. Williams, the attendant, was seeing to that, personally.

All that remained to be wished for was a big Larkland hit for the Partridge Family. It would lift their rapidly-rising star even higher into the musical heavens of rock music.

Jerry Jingo had already been on. Singing and talking the songs that had made him famous and helped him to a fabulous movie career. The crowds had worshipped him. In his tall Stetson and fine dungarees and buckskin shirt, he had brought the house down. If there had been a roof, it would have caved in from the thunderous ocean of acclaim washing in from the audience. Jingo had hit the jackpot on the applause meter.

"Partridge Family! You're on!"

The command came down from the stage as *The Loving Six* trooped off to blistering hand-clapping, whistles and roars of praise. Shirley got the kids lined up, stared at them with shining eyes, and then briskly and proudly murmured: "Okay, kids! Let's show them how it's done."

With that, they tripped up to the stage. Six look-alikes, ready and primed for action, and good music—instruments all set.

Laurie Partridge mounted the platform with stars in her eyes and a song in her young heart. It had to be a great night for the Partridge Family.

As the roars died down, Shirley waved her hands

row,
again.
painted
ily was

Laurie
excitement
tions with
fans. And D
but Laurie wa

"Well, we were
ter Kinkaid tears up ou
one."

"Oh, Danny," Shirley said.
"He's right though," Keith ag

and the guitars throbbed, the drums clicked and all
their voices rose in a unity of harmony, sound, and
tone.

They sang *Lonesome Lonely Me* and it never ever
sounded better. Not in a million times of performance,
or plays on juke boxes. It had a *now* sound, a great
sound, an almost uniquely new sound. The crowd
sensed it, loved it, and they let the Partridge Family
know they knew it.

Larkland's fifty acres literally exploded with applause. The very skies seemed to open up and rain
down thousands of whistles, screams, shouts and tears
of happiness and joy.

There was no doubt about it—Larkland loved the
idge Family!

in their hotel, there was celebra
y had stayed at the Festival until n
to all the great artists, talking to the
nd the campfires, talking with the pr
they would go back and it would start all c
Reuben Kinkaid's smile had been practically
on all night. But now a weary but happy fam-
eady for bed. It had been a long, long day.
was as happy as anybody, but in all the
and confusion, they had missed connec-
Jerry Jingo. He had been mobbed by his
uke had never put in an appearance at all,
sure that she would see him again.

big hit," Danny said. "I hope Mis-
contract and draws a new

How you do go on."
eed. "They really

liked us and we were really good. Funny how you can always tell when you really are *on*—know what I mean, Mom?"

"Uh huh. I sure do. And you're right. I felt it too. We were good tonight. Real good. I was proud of all of you."

Tracy and Christopher yawned so sleepily that Shirley put her foot down and sent everybody off to bed. It was a large suite of rooms and there were beds for everybody even though no one had a room alone. After last night in Satan Hall, Shirley liked it better that way. So Laurie roomed with her.

As they readied themselves for bed, Laurie said, "Mom?"

"Here we go again."

"What do you mean?"

"Everytime you say, 'Mom?' I know you're to ask me another very tough question. So fire aw Just one. I want to sleep."

Laurie sat on her mother's bed and looked at her.

"I'm really too young to be thinking of ge married, aren't I?"

Shirley didn't bat an eye.

"Uh—just a little."

"How long should I wait?" Laurie asked, ous.

"Oh, say two, three years. That would right."

"Gee. That long? You were married early in your life. You couldn't ha eighteen."

"That's about right. Can I

"Sure, Mom, and thank

"You're welcome.

"Good night."

Laurie Partridge lay awake a long time wondering what her children would look like if she married Duke instead of Jerry Jingo. Or Jerry Jingo instead of Duke.

Before she had a satisfactory answer, she was sound asleep.

The suite of rooms was a peaceful bower in the wilderness and wildness of Larkland. But it was the calm before the storm.

The next day began without a hint of trouble.

After a fine breakfast in the coffee shop of the hotel, the family sat around the ornate lobby, reading the Larkland papers which were filled with mentions of their names. Shirley was tickled pink and so were the kids. But Laurie, restless and on edge, asked her mother's permission to take a stroll on the avenue. Shirley consented, with the stern stipulation that she come back within an hour. While her oldest daughter was gone, Shirley intended to get a haircut for Christopher and a manicure for herself. Tracy, Danny, and Keith could baby-sit each other. Keith grumbled about that but in the end gave in. There was a fine camera shop in the lobby of the hotel and he could take a little sister and young Danny in tow while he looked around.

So Laurie walked out on the avenue to window-shop and generally get a breath of fresh air. It was a fine town and a fine day and there were balmy breezes blowing over the nice, clean streets.

Laurie dawdled slowly, going from window to window, thinking about Jerry Jingo and Duke. It was still a neck-and-neck race as far as she was concerned. She just couldn't make up her mind. And then it happened. Just as she was passing a radio repair store, a loudspeaker amplifier which had been playing music for the benefit of passersby, suddenly broke off with a special news announcement: " . . . *screen star Jerry Jingo, attending the Larkland Rock Festival as a Special Guest*, was rushed by private airplane back to *Hollywood early this morning. Jingo had been complaining of stomach cramps to his manager and it is feared he has acute appendicitis. Spurning an offer to be operated on in Larkland Medical Hospital, the singer insisted on being returned to his home in Hollywood where his personal physician will perform the operation. More details later. . . .*"

A Sammy Davis Jr. song came on and Laurie moved down the street in a daze. Gee. Appendicitis. Just like that. And he had looked so hale and hearty only last night! Only yesterday. You just never could tell, could you? Appendicitis—gee, that must hurt!

She hurried along, still thinking about Jerry Jingo and what a bad break it was for the Festival, too. To lose one of its brightest, biggest stars. Maybe the biggest, maybe the brightest—who was bigger and brighter?

The sound of a motorcycle blasting close by made her stop and look up. And it was like a dream come true.

Duke, with sunglasses and crash helmet, was smiling at her from the saddle of his Honda, not more than three feet away.

"Hi," he called.

"Duke! How are you? Where have you been?"

"Guess what," he smiled.

"What?"

"I ran into some real cool cats last night. At the Festival. You were great, by the way. Real great. That mother of yours and the kids are fine musicians. Tell them for me, will you?"

"Sure I will." She stood on the curb, watching him.

He had one booted leg braked to the ground, and he leaned toward her.

"What do you mean about the cool cats?" she asked.

"Bike people. My kind. We're all going to hit the road and head for Hollywood. I'll take Jerry Jingo up on his offer. Guess I could act if I had to."

"You sure could," she answered, but her heart fell. "When will you be going?"

"Got to be tonight. These guys like to keep moving. Two days of the Festival ought to be enough, anyway.

Laurie sighed. "Then you didn't hear about Jerry Jingo on the radio?" He hadn't so she explained it to him. Duke shook his head and sighed. "Well, I'll give him a week to rest up and then I'll hit him with his offer. Unless he was just being grateful at the moment."

"He'll keep his word. Wait and see."

"Okay, I will. Where were you heading just now?"

"No place special. Just walking. Why?"

"Want a ride on my bike?"

"Gee, I'd like to but I'd better not. I've given Mom enough of a headache lately but it is nice of you to ask."

"Suit yourself." Duke smiled.

Laurie was about to say goodbye, but it was meant to be one of those kinds of days where everything happens. A voice behind Laurie suddenly growled. "Well, well, well. Just like I figured. The two love-birds together again!"

She whirled around. There was no mistaking that voice. She'd never forget the first time she'd heard it— in the attic at Satan Hall. She was sure it belonged to the most evil person in all the world.

It was Indian, all right.

The sun glinted off his muscular face and half-bared arms in the warrior vest. The headband on his yellow hair looked silly on Main Street of Larkland—even though there were no passersby and Indian was alone.

Duke climbed off the bike and put the jumpstand down. He stepped between Indian and Laurie. But even so, Laurie backed away in terror.

"What do you want, Indian?" Duke said coolly.

Indian glared back. His eyes were mean.

"I was looking for you. You got to come back. Without you, the others won't hang on. So okay. What do you say?"

"Sorry. I'm moving on."

"No," Indian snarled. "You're coming with me, Duke."

"Yeah? Who's going to make me?" Duke asked.

"I am!"

With that, Indian shot out his right hand into Duke's face. The blow was so sudden and sneaky that Duke had no chance to duck. He slammed up against a fire hydrant and Laurie cried out in horror.

Indian sailed into him and it looked for all the world as though Duke would be beaten to a pulp.

Laurie began to shout for help at the top of her voice.

A CALL FOR HELP

☐ When the phone rang in the Partridge Family suite, a very worried Shirley Partridge sprang to answer it. For more than an hour she had waited for some word from Laurie who had long passed her promised time of return.

Relief flooded Shirley as Laurie's voice came over the wire. "That you, Mom?"

"And where are you, young lady?"

There was a small pause and then Laurie's voice picked up a little in volume.

"Mom, I lost the two men in my life."

"What are you talking about and why are you phoning? Where are you, Laurie Partridge?"

"Give me a minute to explain will you, Mom? It's very important to me. I'm all right. Honest. Now will you listen to me?"

"I'm listening. But you better make it good."

A sigh sounded from the other end of the wire. "I don't know how good it can be?" Laurie's voice broke.

"Laurie, please—"

"You promised you'd listen."

"Oh—all right. Go on."

"Well, first Jerry Jingo got appendicitis. They flew him back to Hollywood for his operation. Can you imagine?"

"Yes. Reuben told me. A very bad break. But what's that to do with you, Laurie?"

"Don't you see? How can I ever see him again? Except in the movies?"

There was another pause before Laurie continued. "And then Duke. That bike means more to him than any girl ever will. He saved our lives but he just isn't the reliable kind. You know what I mean?"

"I know," Shirley said icily, her impatience long since gone. "Now you tell me where you are this minute or I'll never let you out of the house on your own again. And I mean it, young lady!"

"Oh, Mom!"

"Now what?"

"Duke and Indian got in a fight and I yelled for help and the policemen came and now we're all down in the Larkland County Jail. I'm a witness. They're being held for bail and Mom—will you please come down here and get me out of this mess if they promise to reform?"

"I'll be down as fast as Reuben can take me," Shirley answered.

"Gee. That's a relief. Thanks, Mom."

Shirley hung up. The children were playing a big game of Monopoly and Simone was barking again. The Partridges At Home—except Laurie!

She told Keith she was going out for a little while and would be back within the hour. Not much more. Keith waved goodbye to her and when the door had closed he smiled at Danny, Christopher, and Tracy.

"None of you noticed, I suppose."

"Noticed what?" Danny barked, busy collecting an enormous rental from Christopher for landing on Atlantic Avenue.

"That Mom had been crying."

"Is that all?" Danny sniffed. "I know what that means."

"Yes," Tracy said very calmly. "Sister Laurie is being bad again." She rubbed Simone's furry back.

"Will Mom be all right?" Christopher asked.

"Sure," Keith said firmly. "Mom can handle anything."

LARKLAND REMEMBERED

☐ That night under the stars before the same vast assemblage, the Partridge Family went on again, doing their thing and making their wonderful sound. If anything, it was even better than the night before. The country air vibrated with happiness. The Partridge Family created a musical masterpiece of timing and rhythm. The voices, the guitars, the drums, and the tambourines were all inspired. The Festival responded with another avalanche of acclaim. Reuben Kinkaid beamed proudly from platform-side.

Out in the crowds, Indian and Duke, each with a black eye, joined in the celebration. Duke would be on his way by midnight. Indian had accepted that decision, and now the boys were friends.

"Peace from now on, Duke?"

"Sure thing, Indian."

Friendship deepened in the sharing of fun and rock music.

All about Larkland, music filled the air.

Back at Blue Rapids Sanitarium, J. Watterson Turnbull watered the azaleas and Williams looked on closely. Never again would he allow the old man out of his sight when he was his responsibility.

"Williams," J. Watterson Turnbull said, "do you like music?"

"Sure. Guess so. Why?"

"I think I should like to practice playing my guitar again. Those young people I met when I was on my recent trip. They played for me on the way back from the fire. It was a lovely sound. So happy. So bright. It was nearly as good as any fire I've ever heard."

Williams shrugged. "Okay by me, Mr. Watterson. I'll have to ask the Director though.

"Of course."

The old man bent over the azaleas once more with his watering can. Williams shook his head behind Turnbull's back.

You never could tell about old eccentrics, could you?

Play the guitar!

Oh, well, he decided, it certainly was better than playing with matches.

He'd have to remember to ask the Director the next time he saw him about the old man's request. A guitar was harmless enough. It had better be!

Shirley Partridge pulled the big, brightly painted bus into a gas station off the highway. With the Larkland Festival over and the whole affair on the credit side of the ledger, she was anxious to get herself and the kids back home. Reuben Kinkaid had flown back to New York that morning to arrange another busy schedule for the Partridge Family.

Laurie stretched, and then sat up straight when she saw the tall, dark-haired boy working the gas pump. There was something familiar about him. The rest of the kids got out of the bus to stamp the weariness of sitting out of their limbs.

"Mom?"

"Yeah, honey."

"Doesn't that boy look familiar?"

"What boy?"

"The one pumping gas."

Shirley glanced at the attendant at the side of the bus. "Oh, I don't know. Nobody in particular. Why—who were you thinking of?"

Laurie shook her head impatiently. "Don't you see? He looks like Duke. The same intelligent eyes, sensitive mouth—"

"Laurie—"

"And the graceful build. See how he walks?"

"Honey—"

Laurie tilted her chin. "I think it's a remarkable likeness."

"Uh huh." Shirley agreed. "And I'll bet you a dollar to a nickel he also has a motorcycle with which he is madly in love with."

"Oh, I don't know. You can't be sure about a thing like that, can you?"

"So why don't you ask him?"

"All right. I will!"

Shirley turned away to put a coin in the coke vending machine for some soda. Laurie turned to the tall, good-looking boy and smiled at him. He smiled back. He *did* look like Duke. Laurie wished he *was*.

"Hi," she said.

"Hi," he answered back.

"Pardon me for asking but do you own a motorcycle?"

The polite interest on the boy's face evaporated and transformed into sheer rapture.

"Have I? Sweetest little machine you ever saw. Goes up to—"

"That's nice," Laurie Partridge said coldly.

When the bus was rolling down the highway again and everybody back in their seats, Shirley asked, "Well, how did it go?"

"It went," Laurie said glumly. "I don't know how fast. I didn't stay to hear."

Shirley laughed.

The bus sped on, picking up speed, racing toward the sun and the distant horizon of mountains and blue sky.

Keith started playing his guitar. He began to sing *Raindrops Falling On My Head* again. Everybody chimed in—except Laurie. Even Shirley sang from the driver's seat.

They were only about eighteen miles from home and spirits were high. Only Laurie was plunged deep into gloom.

"Come on, Laurie," Danny urged. "Sing. Raise thy golden voice in song."

"Go away."

"Aw, you're a party pooper."

"I am not!"

"You are!"

"I'm not!"

"Children!" Shirley sang out. "You're breaking up the harmony."

"Yeah," Christopher cried. "What do you want to do that for?"

Danny glowered at Laurie and she felt guilty all of a sudden. Everybody sounded so good and she was dragging her feet. Oh, well, she had loved and lost but why let it ruin her young life? So she smiled and sat up and opened her mouth and burst out into song. Keith registered his approval by smiling at her like a Christmas tiger, nodding his head up and down. Tracy giggled at the funny face he made.

Now the bus was filling with all their voices.

"Raindrops falling on my head . . . just like the man whose feet are too big for the bed . . . nothing seems to fit. . . .

The song was wonderful and being a Partridge was wonderful and heck she had her whole life ahead of her. Why worry?

Besides, with haunted houses and fights and fires and all that trouble, the memory of Larkland would probably burn brightly no matter what happened to her from now on.

It had been a beautiful, wonderful time in spite of everything. Something for all the diaries in the universe. And then some.

Yessirree.

Laurie knew—Larkland could never really go away!